Autumn. The worry in his gut cinched one knot tighter.

The door flew open before he reached the porch and a younger version of Autumn with serious blue eyes and red-brown hair stepped out to greet him. The college-aged girl had a streak of blood on her pajama top.

"Autumn?" he choked out, unable to ask the question.

"You're the sheriff? You made good time from town." The girl spun on her heels, gestured to him and led the way toward the brightly lit back door. "Justin and my sister are out there, and they haven't come back."

His knees felt half-jelly as he forced his feet to carry him up the walk. Usually he was invincible, but the thought of Autumn out there facing armed thieves made him weak. He glanced around. Nothing but miles of rangeland and cattle. The paramedics were volunteers from town who were at least twenty minutes away. And a hospital? He had no idea where the closest trauma center would be.

This was a sign. He cared more about Autumn than he'd realized.

Books by Jillian Hart

Love Inspired

*A Soldier for Christmas
*Precious Blessings
*Every Kind of Heaven
*Everyday Blessings
*A McKaslin Homecoming
A Holiday to Remember
*Her Wedding Wish
*Her Perfect Man
Homefront Holiday
*A Soldier for Keeps
*Blind-Date Bride
†The Soldier's Holiday Vow
†The Rancher's Promise
Klondike Hero
†His Holiday Bride

Love Inspired Historical

*Homespun Bride
*High Country Bride
In a Mother's Arms
   "Finally a Family"
**Gingham Bride
**Patchwork Bride

*The McKaslin Clan
†The Granger Family Ranch
**Buttons & Bobbins

JILLIAN HART

grew up on her family's homestead, where she helped raise cattle, rode horses and scribbled stories in her spare time. After earning her English degree from Whitman College, she worked in travel and advertising before selling her first novel. When Jillian isn't working on her next story, she can be found puttering in her rose garden, curled up with a good book or spending quiet evenings at home with her family.

JILLIAN HART

⌐HIS HOLIDAY BRIDE ⌐

Steeple
Hill®

Published by Steeple Hill Books™

STEEPLE HILL BOOKS

Steeple
Hill®

Recycling programs
for this product may
not exist in your area.

ISBN-13: 978-0-373-81503-6

HIS HOLIDAY BRIDE

www.SteepleHill.com

Printed in U.S.A.

My times are in Your hand.

—*Psalms* 31:15

Chapter One

Autumn Granger knew trouble when she saw it, even if she was on the back of a horse riding the crest of a rocky ridge at the tail end of a hard, cold day. She wrapped her scarf tighter around her neck, ignored the wintry bite of wind and focused her binoculars on the cluster of breakaway cattle swarming like flies in the field below.

Hard to tell one cow from another at this distance. Could be Granger stock, but it was impossible to read the brand with the sun slanting low in her eyes. She fished her cell from her pocket and hit speed dial. She was number three man around the ranch. Her older brother Justin would know the scoop.

"Yeah?" he answered, sounding out of breath. He wasn't having an easy afternoon, either.

"Do you have visual on the north Hereford herd?" She swung her binoculars around—nope, still couldn't get a good view—and swept the length of the fence line. Maybe downed barbed wire would tell a better story.

"Dad, Scotty and I are feeding them now. Where are you?"

"The ridge north of the ranch house. Cattle are out." Major bummer.

"I suppose there's a chance they could belong to the Parnells." Justin pondered. "If they turn out to be ours, will you have time to run them in?"

"Already on it." So much for getting off early. That's the way it was when you worked a ranch. The animals came first. She pocketed the phone and dropped the binocs, winding them around her saddle horn. When she drew her Stetson brim down a bit to better shade her face, her bay quarter horse twisted her neck to give an incredulous look.

"I promised you a warm rubdown and a bucket of grain, but we've got to do this." She patted Aggie's nut-brown coat. "Duty calls. Are you with me, girl?"

Aggie nickered a bit reluctantly and started the treacherous descent. Rocks and earth crumbled, speeding ahead of them down the steep slope. Autumn stood in her stirrups, leaning back to balance her weight for Aggie. Winter birds scattered, and in the brush up ahead a coyote skedaddled out of sight. The Grand Tetons marched along the horizon, majestic and purple-blue against the amber crispness of the late November plains. Something in the fields below reflected a blinding streak of light. Strange. She grabbed her binocs and looked again. She focused in until the image came clear. A police vehicle sat sideways in the road as if it had turned a corner, saw the cattle and hit the brakes just in time. Interesting.

That couldn't be the new sheriff, could it? *Lord, please let him know what he's doing. We need a good lawman around here.* The town had brought someone in from out of state, but rumor had it the city slicker hired for the job wouldn't be on until mid-December. Rumors couldn't always be counted on, and maybe this was proof positive. She gave Aggie more rein as the horse slid the last yard to the buffeting clumps of bunch grass below.

"Good girl," she praised, patting her mare's neck. Aggie gave a snort because she knew they would be heading back home the way they came, likely as not. The mare could not be looking forward to climbing up the slope.

Aggie'd had a long day, too. Sympathetic, Autumn lifted her binocs again. This time, she was interested in the cattle. She was close enough to make out the brand.

"Hey, there." A man in a brand new Stetson, black T, Levis and polished riding boots held up a hand in greeting. He stepped away from his four-wheel drive with "Sheriff" in black on the doors and waded through the fallow grasses. "The cows wouldn't happen to be yours, would they?"

"No, sir." She pulled up Aggie, straining to see every last cow flank. "These bear the Parnells' brand."

"Parnell? Sorry, I'm new around here."

"No kidding." When you lived in a small town, strangers stuck out like a sore thumb. "I'm Autumn Granger."

"Good to meet you, Miss Granger. I'm Ford Sherman." He knuckled back his hat to get a better look at her, revealing just about the most hand-some face she'd ever set eyes on. Big blue eyes were striking against his suntanned complexion. His nose was straight and strong but not too big for his face, a complement to the slashing cheekbones and a jaw that would make most male models cry. A day's growth clung to his jawline, a rough tex-ture on a man who was rumored to be city bred.

He was definitely out of place on a Wyoming section road. She wondered how long he would last in these parts. Two weeks, a month before he headed back to urban life?

"I'm trying to find Mustang Road. All I know is that this isn't it." He had a nice grin, friendly and unguarded, but it didn't reach his eyes. Prob-ably a story there, but she didn't care to know it.

Likely as not he wouldn't be around long enough, and besides, whatever it was, it was personal.

She wasn't exactly the type of girl any guy went for. "It's Mustang Lane, and you are about as lost as a soul can get, Sheriff. You need to backtrack to the main county road. Stay on the pavement until you hit the other side of our spread."

"And I would know that how?"

"It's the first intersecting road you come to. You have a dazed look on your face. Where are you from?"

"Chicago."

"I'm guessing you haven't seen so much open land except in an old Western?"

"I noticed it on the plane when I flew out to interview, but I kept close to town. Didn't get a chance to wander off the main street."

"Out here it's mostly ranches, rangeland and cattle. You've got to keep on eye on cows, or don't you know? They're going to tear your vehicle apart."

"What?" He whipped around. Sure enough, the mammoth black-and-white creatures had abandoned their grazing to gnaw on his four-wheel drive. They clustered around it like a mob, mouths and tongues and teeth bent on destruction. One cow tried to pry the wiper off the windshield, another chewed on the side-view mirror. Several leaned through the open window licking the seats.

Another pulled a clean T-shirt out of his duffel and waved it in the wind like a prize.

"Shoo!" He didn't know the first thing about cattle in real life, but he'd read plenty of Westerns where they were easy to scare into a stampede— not that he wanted a stampede, but this was a dire situation. He was responsible for that vehicle. How was he going to explain teeth marks to the town council? "Get up. Move along, little dogie."

The entire herd swiveled their heads in unison to study him curiously. Not one of them was the least bit scared. Not a single hoof shifted. The animals returned to chewing, licking and digging through his possessions as if he were no threat at all.

"Move along, little dogie?" The woman on the horse laughed, a warm and wonderful sound. She dropped her reins, her hands at her stomach, watching him as if he was the funniest thing she'd ever seen. "That was a good one. I needed that."

"Glad to help out." He might be inexperienced with cows, but he understood hard work. "Tough day?"

"Tough and long." She swiped her eyes. "Sorry, didn't mean to poke fun at you. Do you know *anything* about cattle?"

"Not in real life." There was a lot he could tell her, but he didn't. He rather liked the way she watched him with a crook of a grin and a look as if to say she had seen this before. Let her think what she wanted. He gave his hat a tug and turned his attention to her. "I read a lot of Westerns. Or, I did when my granddad was alive. He got me hooked on them. We would sit and read side by side for hours at a time."

"You must miss him."

"He passed on about eight years back, and yeah, I still miss him."

"I know how that is." She'd lost her mom when she'd been in high school, and then her grandparents died one by one. It was the cycle of life— birth and death, love and grief—turning like the seasons, unable to be stopped. "Next time you come across cows in the road, you have to consider what you're dealing with. Range cattle are used to being herded. Pets are not."

"And what I've got here are pets?"

"Parnell has four daughters and 4-H animals galore. Watch and learn." She reined her horse toward the herd.

A cutting horse, he realized, a beautiful creature with a dark brown coat and a long silky black mane and tail. An American quarter horse, pedigreed, by the looks of those fine lines. Considering the dishpan profile, the wide, intelligent eyes and the impeccable conformation, his guess was a very well-pedigreed mare. Even more beautiful was the woman in command, sitting straight in the saddle as if she'd been born to ride. Woman and horse sliced through the middle of the swarm. Autumn Granger pulled something out of the pack tied behind her saddle.

"Look what I have, guys. Cookies." Wintry sunshine burnished her strawberry-blond hair as she held up a sandwich bag and rattled it.

Cows swung in her direction, abandoning the mirrors, the bumpers and his luggage. Dozens of liquid brown eyes brightened with excitement as she opened the bag and shook it again. The enticing scent of homemade snickerdoodles carried on the wind, and even his stomach growled.

"Follow me." She circled around the car. The cattle bounded after her, and the earth shook with the force of their powerful hooves.

"It was nice meeting you, Sheriff." She tipped her hat. She looked awesome and powerful on the back of that horse, but up close it surprised him to see that she was petite and fragile. For all her presence, she was a bit of a thing with a heart-shaped face and delicate features, big, hazel eyes and a sugar-sweet smile. Slim and graceful, she leaned closer. "Don't worry, they'll go around you. This isn't a rampaging stampede."

"Where are you taking them?"

"Back to the Parnells. Easiest route is the road." She glanced over her shoulder. "You had best stop off at the feed store and tell Kit at the counter you need molasses treats to keep in your rig. Next time you'll be on your own, city boy."

The enormous creatures broke around him, their heads upraised, sniffing the air, their eyes bright with cookie hopes. They dashed around him, shaking the ground and jarring his teeth, and then they were gone, obscured by the rising cloud of dust like something out of an old cowboy movie. But it wasn't the cows he missed. The cowgirl stayed on his mind, the sweetest thing he had ever seen. He pulled the keys from his pocket, rescued two shirts from the ground and stalked over to his rig.

Autumn ended the call and tucked her cell into her pocket. Parnell would send someone over. The cattle would be taken care of soon. *If* there wasn't a single problem getting home and she sped through Aggie's care and a super-fast shower, she *might* make it into town to meet her friends on time. Maybe. She could only hope at this point. The work day wasn't done yet, and who knew what would happen next?

A cow's sharp moo broke into her thoughts. What was wrong now? She twisted in her saddle. The bulk of the cattle were following her, straining for the cookie bag, but the ones in the back glanced behind them nervously. Another heifer took to lowing in protest. And could she blame them?

Not one bit. The new sheriff had caught up with them. He trailed behind the herd in his Jeep, strobes flashing. What was the man thinking?

"You are going to wear out those lights," she called above the plod of three dozen cattle.

"Miss Granger, you and the cows are a traffic hazard." He leaned out the window, his dark hair tousled by the wind. "I don't want anyone to get hurt, so I'm escorting you."

"Turn the lights off. They are giving me a headache and the cows aren't liking it."

"Sorry, no can do. It's procedure."

"I can keep this herd together if they bolt, but I'd rather not work Aggie that hard. She's had a long day, too."

"I don't want to get fired. The lights stay on."

"Don't you know better than to argue with a woman who's packing?" Not that she would shoot him or anyone—the Colt .45 she carried was strictly for frightening off wildlife and the occasional rattler—but it was fun to see the question pass across his face.

"You've got a permit for that?"

A permit? Autumn found herself grinning wider. He wasn't too bad for an outsider, especially when he cut the lights. Nope, not a bad guy at all. The big question was how long he would last before he went the way of three out of the last four lawmen who'd held his job. They'd run back to city life as fast as they could bolt.

She rode along, attention on the cattle. The animals closest to her held their heads up and their tongues out, trying to hook the cookie bag. When she hit the main road, she leaned right and led the herd along the pavement. Out of the corner of her eye, she caught the sheriff's SUV ambling the wrong way in the oncoming lane, headlights bright to warn any approaching traffic.

A little overkill, considering the only vehicle they came across was Jeremy Miller in his semi-sized tractor rumbling toward them at a leisurely clip. Autumn waved when Jeremy did.

"Who's the yahoo with the lights?" The rancher leaned out his window.

"The new sheriff."

"Just my luck. I didn't think he was supposed to start until December."

"Neither did I." She glanced over her shoulder. The sheriff had eased back behind her to give the tractor his lane. "Did you see Parnell back there?"

"Spotted two of his girls riding down the hill. They ought to catch up with you in a few." Jeremy tipped his Stetson and raised his window, so that air conditioning and satellite radio kept him comfy and entertained as he rolled along. She suspected he waved to the sheriff, but she didn't look to be sure.

I give him three months tops before he heads back to Chicago, she thought, glancing over her shoulder. Yep, there he was back in the oncoming lane, trying to keep the cattle from drifting over into it, determined to protect the ranching population of White Horse County from a few cows on a rangeland road. Poor guy. Probably really thought he was helping.

She spotted the Parnell girls on the next rise. Both high school girls trotted along the road, horses' manes flying. When they were closer, one of them—Ashleigh—held up a small pail and rattled it. "Grain!"

Cow heads swung higher. The promise of cookies was forgotten as excited moos rang out and the three dozen animals took off at an eager lope.

"Thanks, Autumn!" Hazel called out.

"No problem." She drew Aggie to a stop and rested her hands on the pommel. The saddle's leather was cool from the near-freezing temperature.

"Is that the new sheriff?" Ashleigh asked.

"So I'm told." Behind her she heard a door whisk open and an engine idling.

"I didn't know he was in town already. Cool."

The girls wheeled their mounts and took off, trailed by their pets, who raced after them.

"Why *are* you here?" Autumn urged Aggie around to face the newcomer. "It's not December."

"Came early to get settled in. I'm not officially on the clock yet. The mayor told me I could have the car for personal use. Part of my salary."

"That and you're the only officer around, so you get to answer all the emergency calls. Even in the middle of the night. Did he tell you that?"

"I heard a fleeting mention. The mayor made it sound like it was no big deal. Do emergency calls come in a lot around here?"

"I have no idea." She dismounted with a creak of the saddle and the thud of her boots on the road. *Couldn't be more than five foot three,* he decided. She stood a full foot shorter than he did.

"Is there anything else I should know? Wait. Maybe I don't want to hear it. Maybe next you'll be telling me Miller's rental house is really a henhouse." Couldn't say why he felt the need to tease another smile from her, but he did.

"No, but it *is* a barn."

"What?" He'd only been joking. His pulse screeched to a stop. A barn? He'd trusted the real estate agent, who was the mayor's wife. "That's what I get for renting sight unseen."

"You figured you could trust us honest country folk, right?" Her hazel eyes, an amazing combination of browns, greens and golds twinkled like veiled trouble.

He didn't think she was laughing at him, but she was having fun with him. He had the feeling he wasn't the first city boy who'd come to these parts and had decided to banter with the pretty cowgirl. *Very* pretty, he corrected. So pretty that he'd like to get to know her more.

"Living in a barn won't be so bad." She turned to her saddle pack and dug through the leather bag. "Think of it this way. Because of all the animals, you will always have company. You'll get the full country experience. Plus, you won't have to pack water far at all, since there's an outside pump nearby."

"Pump?" That didn't sound like the place had indoor plumbing. "Are you serious? No, you're kidding me."

"You read all those Westerns. You ought to know about ranch life." She handed him a roll of duct tape. "It's probably illegal to drive without a functioning side-view mirror. Good luck, Sheriff."

"Do you want to have dinner with me?"

"Nope. I'm busy tonight." That was an urban dude for you, always eager to play the dating game.

"Any night, then. How about Friday?"

"Can't. Busy then, too." She swung into the

saddle, settled into the stirrups and considered the man leaning against the side of his four-wheel-drive. He was trying to look suave while clutching a roll of tape and standing next to a dangling mirror. The cows had not been kind to the vehicle. "Here's a hint. Country girls aren't dumb or easy. Have a good evening."

"I never thought—"

She pressed her heels to Aggie's side and the mare took of, eager for the day to be over, too. Autumn tipped her hat as they raced by. This wasn't her first experience with a city sheriff come to town.

I don't know about that guy, she told herself, leaning forward in her saddle as Aggie's gait changed to a canter. Sheriff Ford Sherman might not be Denny Jones, but he may as well be.

The drum of Aggie's steel shoes became pleasant music to match the wind whistling in her ears as they raced home.

Chapter Two

A barn? Not only was Ford surprised to learn the tractor guy was his landlord, but his new dwelling was a barn. Imagine that. The pretty cowgirl hadn't been pulling his leg after all.

"Ought to have everything you need," Jeremy Miller was saying as he paced across the bars of sunshine from the front window and dropped the keys on the windowsill. "Except furniture. You got a truck coming? If not, I could put in a call to the furniture store over in Sunshine. It's the closest big town around until you hit Jackson."

"I've got a moving truck coming with my stuff."

"Good luck with that." Jeremy tipped his Stetson and lumbered toward the open door where a fly buzzed in. "Took the liberty of getting the phone company out here to set you up. Should be here day after tomorrow. My cousin works for the company and squeezed you in."

"That was thoughtful of you, Jeremy. Thanks."

"No problem. Least I can do for the new sheriff. Just do me a favor, will ya?" Miller halted on the porch. "Give me some notice before you bolt."

"Bolt?" Like leave?

"When you've had enough of small town life. It'll happen, don't you worry. You're not the first sheriff I've rented to."

That didn't bode well. What was wrong with the job he didn't know about? Learning from Autumn Granger that maybe the emergency calls came in more often than he'd been led to believe had thrown him. Maybe he'd made a mistake burning the bridges of his old life to come here.

I hope this isn't one of those impulsive decisions I live to regret, Lord.

"Give me a call if you need anything." Jeremy bobbed his head in a single nod—a gesture of goodbye, country style.

Ford did the same, his movements echoing in the wide open space of the living area. Outside the slam of a truck's door ricocheted like a bullet through the quiet and a pickup's motor turned over and rumbled away.

Alone in his new place, he paced across the high-gloss oak floor and stared out the bay window. The horse barn had been totally remodeled with sedate gray siding, white trim, ivory walls and indoor plumbing. He batted at the lone fly, smiling as he thought of Autumn Granger. He did not know what to think about the woman, but he liked her. Hard not to like a gal who carried a holstered .45 at her hip and a lasso on her saddle.

Granddad would have loved seeing all this. Ford frowned, shaking his head. Too bad he hadn't made this change earlier, when his grandfather had been alive and he'd been more optimistic about his life.

Regrets. He shrugged them off. A pack of cows was grazing out beyond the small patch of lawn behind red posts and three skinny strands of barbed wire. He saw one of them eyeing his Jeep and hoped to high heaven those animals didn't get out and gnaw something else off the poor vehicle. One of the first things on his list would be to drop by the feed store for treats. Without them, he feared the Jeep wouldn't last long.

His stomach rumbled. That got him thinking about dinner. Maybe he would mosey down the street and see what he could rustle up.

"What are you still doing here?"

"Good question." Autumn leaped over the last two stairs, landed in the kitchen and grabbed her purse off the table by the back door. She tossed a grin at Rori, her friend, the family's temporary housekeeper and her older brother's fiancée. "I'm about an hour late. My friends are going to disown me."

"You? Never." Rori hefted a big pan of pasta over the sink and upended it. Water and noodles tumbled into a steel colander. "Have fun."

"I intend to." For a change. First it had been calving and foaling season, then it had been harvest and hay. "The last time I had a free night in town it was February."

"The life of a rancher. Why exactly did you want to do this for a living?"

"No idea. Must have been out of my mind." She found her truck keys in a drawer, wished Rori a good night and flew out the door.

"Whoa there, little lady." Her dad, Frank Granger, caught her before she charged into him. "Where are you off to in such a hurry?"

"It's my night off, remember?"

"I didn't know you were allowed one of those." He chuckled. That was her dad, Mr. Humor.

"Ha, ha. I won't be out too late, but don't wait up." She danced around him, skipping down the porch steps, two at a time.

"You've got a four-thirty wake-up call, girl."

"I know!" As if she could forget. She'd been waking up that early as long as she could remember. Really. Dad must think he was hilarious. She could be a comedian, too. "Hey, guess who I'm giving a riding lesson to on Saturday?"

"Uh, are you still doing that?" Frank swept off his Stetson. Something passed across his rugged face that looked a lot like interest.

Yeah, that's just what she'd thought. She kept going, running backwards. "Cady Winslow. The nice lady new to town who bought one of my horses? You remember her, right?"

"I suppose." He cast his gaze down, as if looking at some trouble with one of the porch boards.

Good way to hide his interest, but she wasn't fooled. She tripped along the concrete path. "You could drop by the arena tomorrow if you want. Hang around. Offer some advice."

"I'm sure you've got it covered." A faint blush crept high on his face. "Have a good time tonight, darlin'."

"Sure." That was the problem with men in this family. They didn't give much away. They acted as if real feelings were something to be wrestled down and extinguished.

"Autumn, you know we've got an early morning tomorrow." Her older brother Justin called out as he slipped between the fence boards. "Don't be too late."

"Late is the story of my life." The dinner bell on the back porch clanged, signaling the time as she hauled open the garage door. Six o'clock. Late,

late, late. Her friends were used to it. She'd been leaving them to order for her for years.

She jammed the key into the ignition, turned over the engine and took the driveway as fast as she dared. Gravel crunched beneath the tires and dust rose up in her back trail, blocking all views of the pretty two-story ranch house tucked between the orchard and a copse of aspen.

The second she hit the county road, images of the new sheriff dogged her. His wide-shouldered stance. The dimples bracketing his grin. Confidence beaming from him like the sun from above. Gorgeous. She was a total softy when it came to a man with dimples and big baby blues. A sign she couldn't give this man an inch. She gave the truck a little more juice, ignored the posted speed limit by a few miles per hour and kept an eye out for wildlife and livestock.

The trick was to keep the to-die-for new sheriff out of her mind. She glanced at the dashboard clock—eight minutes after six. Yikes. A hawk swooped low in the road in front of the truck. She hit the brakes to miss it. The creature sailed away, and in that unguarded moment her thoughts returned to Ford Sherman. She would never forget the look on his face when he realized the cows were destroying his Jeep. *That's something you don't get in a Western movie,* she thought.

If only she could have witnessed the look on his

face when he saw his remodeled barn. That would have been priceless. No doubt he was mighty relieved to discover he had indoor plumbing and not a single barnyard animal sharing his living quarters.

The radio blared, and Christian country songs accompanied her all the way to town. She skidded into a spot in front of the diner, leaped out of her truck and hit the ground running. After she popped through the front door and glanced at the clock behind the till, she wanted to pump her fist in the air. She'd shaved two minutes off her drive time.

"There she is." Merritt waved from a booth halfway down the long stretch of front window. "I can't believe my eyes. She's here almost on time."

"*Before* we had to order for her." Caroline twisted around to wave, too. "Glad you could make it. We figured you got held up on the ranch."

"Broken fence line, escaped cattle, met the new sheriff. I didn't think I would make it, but Scotty offered to take care of Aggie for me." Bless their best hired man. She dropped into the booth beside Caroline. "Otherwise, I'd still be in the stables. How have you been?"

"Let's go back to the part about you meeting the new sheriff." Merritt flipped a lock of brown hair over her shoulder and leaned one elbow on the table. "So, spill. Is he young or old?"

"Cute or ugly?" Caroline took a sip of soda.

"He's somewhere in this thirties." She grabbed the laminated menu and flipped it open. "Not too ugly, I guess."

"Well, he at least sounds promising—" Merritt fell silent, her sentence unfinished. Her eyes rounded.

A battered roll of duct tape landed on the edge of the table, held in place by a sun-browned hand. The hand was attached to a muscled arm, and she didn't have to look farther to know who belonged to that arm. Ford Sherman.

"Not too ugly?" His baritone warmed with amusement.

Okay, not the most comfortable situation she'd ever been in. Good going, Autumn. She squirmed on the vinyl bench seat, wishing she could disappear beneath the table, spontaneously combust, anything to escape the embarrassment. She'd wanted to hide her interest in him, that was all. What she needed was a snappy comeback. "What do you think, girls? We have certainly seen worse in these parts."

Not a snappy comeback, but the best she could do under the circumstances.

"Worse?" Ford's gaze latched onto hers, an intense, uncomfortable probing that only made his dimples deepen. "You think because I'm from the city I can't measure up?"

"No, I was talking solely about your appearance."

"Good to know." Judging by the twinkle in the sheriff's knowing eyes, he wasn't offended.

"Did the tape help? Or is your side mirror still dangling in the wind?"

"It is fixed for now." He released his hold on the roll and stepped back, giving her the once-over. He'd thought her magnificent on her horse with the sun at her back, framed by a perfect blue sky. But without her Stetson, her strawberry-blond hair tumbled around her face and shoulders in a soft cascade. Her features were scrubbed clean, her complexion perfect. She was girl-next-door wholesome in an ivory sweater and jeans. He liked this side of her, too. "You clean up nice, Miss Granger. Very nice. I almost didn't recognize you without your .45."

"I only wear it when I'm working. Usually there's no need to scare off varmints in the diner."

"I hope you're not hinting that I'm a varmint."

"Who, me?"

He liked her sense of humor, too. Out of the corner of his vision, he spied the waitress setting his burger and fries on the corner table in the back. "I'm keeping my eye on you, Miss Granger.

Something tells me you are trouble waiting to happen."

"Me, trouble?"

The young women at the table began to laugh. "It's true," the black-haired woman said. "Disaster finds you, Autumn."

"Trouble has always been her middle name," the brown-haired one agreed merrily.

"I'm not that bad." Autumn had a cute gleam in her eye.

He lifted his hand in farewell, reluctant to turn around and walk away, but he didn't want to keep blocking the aisle. He couldn't explain the spark of interest in her or the weighing disappointment as he turned on his heel and left her behind.

"He's not ugly," Merritt whispered over ice cream sundaes. "I've thought about it all through the meal, and I can't see it. You don't think he's gorgeous?"

This was not what she wanted to discuss, thanks. Autumn took a big bite of syrup-covered ice cream, knowing full well the sting of brain pain was coming. But did she care?

No. Bring on the agony. It was better than having to admit the truth to her friends.

"He's a hunk." Caroline licked the syrup off her spoon.

"A hunky hunk."

"Fine. So he's gorgeous." She rubbed her forehead—ow—and kept her voice low. No way was she going to take the risk that their conversation might carry across the noisy Friday night crowd to Ford Sherman's no doubt supersensitive ears. Everything about him looked superior, why not his hearing?

"Then he's all yours." Caroline plunged her spoon into her butterscotch sundae. "I think he likes you."

"Why do you say that?" He couldn't like her. He didn't know her.

"Because he keeps stealing glances this way, and he's not looking at me." Caroline stirred her sundae around. "That's it, I'm stuffed."

"Me, too." Merritt gave up on her dessert with a sigh.

Autumn scraped the bottom of the glass bowl with her spoon and licked the last drop of fudge. After divvying up the check, leaving a pile of bills and change on the table, they filed out of the booth and down the aisle. It took all her willpower not to glance over her shoulder. She didn't have to look to know Ford was watching her. The force of his gaze settled on her back like a dead weight. Best to ignore it.

The crisp evening air greeted her as she ambled along the sidewalk. A motorcycle rumbled down the road, the only traffic on the street. A dog barked somewhere on the residential blocks behind the diner. The nape of her neck tingled. Was the sheriff tracking her as she passed in front of the window?

"Something's wrong with your truck." Caroline noticed it as she set her purse on the hood of her car. "Your tire is flat."

"All of them are." Merritt squinted at the damage.

"What?" She'd been so busy wondering about Ford that she hadn't noticed her truck. Deflated rounds of rubber sagged tiredly against the pavement, all the air gone. She'd never seen such flat tires. Had she run over something in the road? She knelt to get a good look, and her heart slammed to a stop. A neat cut sliced the upper curve of the front tire.

A slice, not a nail or a screw or anything like that. Someone had done this on purpose. Judging by the size of the gash, whoever had done this must have used a bowie knife.

"It's the same back here." Merritt had spotted the slit in the back tire. "Who would do something like this? We were close by the whole time."

"I should have seen it from my seat." Should have, yes. Why hadn't she? Because she spent the whole meal fixated on the new sheriff and trying not to be, there had been little attention left over to notice anything other than her friends. What had happened to her decision not to think about him?

"We are currently sheriff-less, right?" Caroline shrugged, glancing down the road to the closed up sheriff's office. "The old guy is gone, and the hunky one isn't officially at work yet. So do we bother him? Who do we call?"

"No idea. I need Loren and his wrecker." Shock pulsed through her in little beats. *Lord, I know You're in charge but who would have done such a thing? And why?* She swallowed, pulling her thoughts together. She needed a working truck. Loren had the only tow truck in thirty-five miles. "Here's hoping he has the right tires in stock."

"I can give you a lift home," Merritt spoke up.

"Thanks." She couldn't stop staring at the knife slit. Wild Horse was a small town and a friendly one. There wasn't a whole lot of crime. Few people in these parts would disable a ranch truck. She couldn't think of a single person who would.

"Is there a problem, ladies?" Ford ambled out of the diner.

"A small one." Of course, it would have to be him.

"Let me take a look." He eased down next to her, squinting hard at the knife slash. "Looks like you've got trouble here. Is there anything you want to tell me about?"

"Like what?"

"Crazy ex-boyfriend, a long-standing feud, someone who has a grudge against you?"

"Not for a long time, no, and not that I know of." She swiped a lock of red-gold hair out of her eyes. "This is deliberate. No one else's tires are slashed."

"I noticed." Considering every car on the street was clustered around the diner, it was obvious. He knelt down to take a closer look at the angry gash in the rubber. Someone sure didn't like Autumn. "Anything unusual happen lately?"

"Nothing out of the ordinary, except for meeting you."

Was that a hint of a grin on her lips? He wasn't prepared for the sight of Autumn smiling. He was a professional, even if he wasn't on the clock yet. If he wasn't careful, he was going to have unprofessional thoughts about her centering on conversation with candlelight and a nice steak. She'd turned him down once, but she hadn't sounded one hundred percent final. There had been a glimmer in her eyes.

"I didn't do this, as you know. I also have an alibi." He slipped the paperback he carried into his rear pocket. "I was in the thick of Larry McMurtry. But I'll find out who did."

"If someone saw something, they would have said so. This isn't a big city. People don't look the other way here." Her gaze met his, and the force of it was like the sun and moon colliding. Hard to think straight when such a pretty woman was waiting for an intelligent remark. It was even harder to pretend he was stone-cold granite, professional and unaffected.

"Hey, you! What's going on over there?" someone called out. A shadow fell across him. Ford looked up to see an elderly man with his wife at his side hurrying along the sidewalk. Fearless, the gray-haired stranger shook his finger angrily. "What are you doing to that truck? Get away—oh, howdy, Autumn. I didn't see you there."

"Hi, Mr. and Mrs. Plum." Autumn's smile of welcome was one of greeting for old friends. She rose, the tires forgotten. "This is our new sheriff. He's your neighbor, too."

"Howdy." Ford climbed to his feet.

"Oh. Mighty fine to meet you, sir." The older man had a powerful stance, a direct gaze and a firm handshake. "Velma and I thought we saw someone at Miller's rental place, but we didn't look too close. It could have been the Realtor."

"Martha's been in and out now and again showing the place. Didn't know it was let." Velma Plum patted his hand in a motherly welcome. "If I'd known, I would have had an apple crisp ready for you. I'd best get crackin'. Hal, remind me when we get home. You know how I am—"

"Always stopping to chat with everyone. Always talking away and losing track of everything else." Hal winked, as if he didn't mind at all. When he gazed at his wife, it was with great, accepting love. "Look, there's Betty. See what I mean?"

"I see." Ford watched a woman in her fifties greet Velma with a hug. Both of the women fell to talking.

"Need a hand there, young fella?" Hal asked.

"What I need is information. You wouldn't have noticed anyone slinking around this truck, would you?"

"Besides you?" Hal quipped.

Autumn's amusement hit him like a wind gust. He could feel her holding back laughter. More folks came out of the diner to congregate on the sidewalk, already discussing the slashed tires.

Looked like she was right. Apparently, little went unnoticed in a small town.

Chapter Three

"Autumn!"

Somewhere far away in the dark she heard her name, but it wasn't powerful enough to yank her out of her dream. Her bed was warm and her electric blanket cozy, and in her mind she was at the diner running her spoon through the hot fudge and trying not to feel a pull in Ford's direction.

Keep your attention on the ice cream, she told herself. *Ice cream is better for you, calories and all, than he is. Dudes are nothing but heartache.*

"Autumn!" A full-fisted pounding rattled her bedroom door. "Wake up!"

"Dad?" The dream evaporated and she sat up. Her pillow tumbled to the floor, she kicked off her covers and rubbed her eyes. Cool air enveloped her. The numbers on the clock shone blurrily in the ink-dark room. She squinted, bringing them into focus. Two-forty-three. What was going on?

Then she heard it: a faint, rhythmic, rapid-fire sputtering. A helicopter.

"We got trouble," Dad shouted, moving on down the hall to pound on Cheyenne's door. "Up and at 'em!"

Rustlers. Her feet hit the floor and she grabbed her clothes from last night, pulling them on as she went. By the time she threw open her door, she was only missing shoes. She'd grab her boots on her way through the mudroom.

In the hall up ahead, Dad hammered on the last door—Addison's—before racing downstairs. She jammed her bare feet into her riding boots and grabbed her cell from her purse.

"Here." Frank handed her a rifle and a box of cartridges. His phone rang and he answered it, grabbing a second rifle. "I just put a call in to the sheriff and the county. They said they'd be here in ten to twenty. They've got the only chopper aound, and it will take a while to get in the air."

Rifle in hand, she flew out the door and into the night. Surrounded by darkness and shadows, she ignored the nearby cow mooing plaintively, wondering what was going on, and hit the ground running. She ate up distance, whistling for Aggie. The *whop-whop* grew louder. She could see the faint flash of a helicopter's safety lights above the far hillside's crest before the vehicle nosed down to make another pass. No doubt it was rounding up their animals and scaring them into a hard run. She prayed the Lord was watching over the livestock.

Aggie nickered, hooves pounding the dirt as she skidded to a stop. No time to bridle up. Autumn ripped open the gate, caught Aggie by a handful of mane and leaped. She landed on her mare's back as the horse broke into a hard gallop. They rode in sync, bulleting up the gravel road that stretched from the house to the long row of barns, stables and outbuildings.

Dad was behind her, calling for Rogue. His cutting horse answered with an anxious whinny. In the shadows, she caught sight of her sisters dashing full speed from the house. She searched the darkness ahead. Where was Justin? Best guess, he was headed for the rustlers.

She wheeled Aggie toward the hillside, leaning low and urging the mare into a hard canter. She heard an engine flare to life, and a headlight pierced the darkness. Justin. Halfway up the hill, her dad on Rogue passed her. No time to say anything, but she knew her father's plan. She gripped the gun tightly in her right hand and prayed she wouldn't have to use it.

The helicopter wheeled around to make another pass, and gunfire flashed from the loading door.

Bullets zinged through the air, biting into rock and earth and kicking up dust all around them. Aggie didn't startle but put her head down with determination, her hooves eating up ground.

Up ahead, both Dad on horseback and Justin on the ATV ground to a halt. Her dad was fast, sighting and firing first. Must have been a hit, because the rustler's semiautomatic fired in a fast burst, bullets licking haphazardly along the hillside away from them before falling silent. The helicopter went nose up and ate distance.

"They're not done with us yet," Frank shouted. "You girls split up. Addison and Cheyenne, go with Justin along the section line."

"I'm with you, Dad." She signaled Aggie around to the field gate and unlatched it, backing the horse to swing it wide. "You didn't take a bullet this time, did you?"

"No. Don't you worry about me, missy." He flashed a grin as he raced past her. "You stay behind me, you hear?"

That was her dad, always taking the lead, fearless, although years ago he'd taken two bullets to the chest chasing off rustlers. If the county's helicopter hadn't been on site and flown him straight to the hospital at Jackson, they would have lost him.

Please keep protecting him, she prayed, clinging to Aggie as the horse lunged up the dark, treacherous slope. Rocks rolled, earth shifted and Aggie lost her footing. For one terrible second Autumn felt them tumbling backwards. She leaned forward, resisting the instinct to dismount, and stuck with her horse.

Aggie pawed her way back onto the trail and surged forward until they were on solid ground again. Grateful, Autumn wiped grit from her face, ignored the adrenaline spiking through her system and focused on following her dad along the ridge. The helicopter, farther away now, made one low sweep. Another shot rang out in their direction. Before she could hit the safety and lift her rifle, bullets whizzed by and dirt and rock flew. Something hit her in the leg—a slight sting. A rock sliver. Her dad got off another shot before the helicopter wheeled low and began to smoke.

"Got 'em." He sounded grim. "Trouble is, I think they got me, too."

It was strange to be woken out of a sound sleep by the dispatch operator and to hear the words, "Cattle rustlers." Ford felt like he was sleepwalking through an old cowboy movie as he jumped into clothes and his Jeep. Lights flashing, he barreled through the sleeping town and along the rolling countryside, startling owls and coyotes as he broke speed barriers following directions to a ranch off Mustang Lane.

Good thing he knew where Mustang Lane was. That brought up images of the pretty red-haired cowgirl he'd taken a shine to—now he was *thinking* like an old Western. Made it seem even more like a dream until he spotted the address he was looking for on a big black mailbox and the last name spelled out in silver reflective letters. *Granger.*

Autumn's ranch. Fear gripped his gut as he gunned it, taking the gravel drive at a fast clip. It wove between a shadowed copse of trees and up a rise. Up ahead a two-story house perched, windows glowing like a beacon in the night. He followed the driveway to the side of the house and a detached garage with six doors. He hit the brakes, launched out of his seat and followed the porch light to the back of the house.

The door flew open before he reached the porch and a younger version of Autumn with serious blue eyes and red-brown hair stepped out to greet him. The college-aged girl had a streak of blood on her pajama top.

"Autumn?" He choked out, unable to ask the question. The fear in his gut cinched tight.

"You're the sheriff? You made good time from town." The girl spun on her heels, gestured to him and led the way toward the brightly lit back door. "Justin and my sister are out there, and they haven't come back."

His knees felt half-jelly as he forced his feet to carry him up the walk. Usually he was invincible, but the thought of Autumn out there facing armed thieves made him weak. He glanced around. Nothing but miles of rangeland and cattle. The paramedics were volunteers from town who were at least twenty minutes away. And a hospital? He had no idea where the closest trauma center would be.

This was a sign. He cared more about Autumn than he'd realized. He stumbled up the steps, across the porch and into the bright lights of a spacious kitchen.

"You must be Ford Sherman." A brawny man in his early fifties sat at a round oak table with his chair pushed back, T-shirt sleeve rolled up and fresh sutures exposed. He stood and extended his good hand. "Glad to meet you. I'm Frank Granger."

"Looks like you've been better." They shook. He'd seen a wound like that before. "You took a bullet."

"Flesh wound, mostly." Granger didn't look troubled by it.

"Dad, sit down." Another red-haired young woman pointed to the chair and scowled at him. "You've been shot."

"Yeah, but it's not bad."

"I don't care. You're going to sit down and stay

down." This daughter, who looked to be somewhere in her mid-twenties, dabbed a swab along
tidy stitches, her stern tone at odds with the affection on her face. "You could have been killed."

"Nothing vital got hit."

"You still could have slipped off your horse,
rolled down the ridge and died, so you will stay
in this chair or I'll rope you into it." She dropped
the swab into a wastebasket and reached for a
sealed package of gauze. "I'm almost as good as
Autumn when it comes to calf roping, so don't
tempt me."

"Women." Frank shook his head, good-natured,
as he eased back into his chair and turned to the
business at hand. "Out in the field, I got a few
good shots in. Didn't see a fireball, but I probably
forced them down. If I did, they couldn't have
gone far. They've got an injured man with them
and likely one on the ground."

"I haven't been briefed on all this." As a country
lawman, he was out of his depth. Back in Chicago
they would set up a perimeter and start a search.
"Anyone else hurt?"

"Don't know. Haven't heard from Justin, my
oldest son. He's either out of cell range or in a
lick of trouble. Since I haven't heard gunshots,
I'm guessing he and Autumn are safe."

Autumn. The worry in his gut cinched one
notch tighter.

"Ow, Cheyenne." Granger winced and yanked his arm away. "Aren't you done yet? I gotta go."

"Do I need to get a lasso?" the daughter threatened.

"Honey, you go right on ahead, but remember this. You can't outrun me." Frank winked, rolled down his sleeve and bounded to his feet. "C'mon, sheriff. Let's go huntin'. You know how to ride a horse?"

"I'll manage."

"That's the spirit." Granger opened a cabinet and tossed him a rifle. "You'll need this. That little Glock you're packing might not do the trick."

Ford's fingers closed on the cold metal stock, and he clicked into action mode. The setting might be different, but the task was the same. This was what he knew. This was what he was good at. He led the way out the door, down the steps and into the night.

"I can't believe this." Autumn rode up alongside her brother on the ridge. Below rolled the shadowed meadows and lowland hills, and a herd of quarter horses huddled in the hollows. "You walked up here?"

"As fast as my boots could carry me." His grip tightened on the binocs. "Had a blowout. Someone knifed the tires. I was lucky to get as far as I did."

"Puts a whole new light on what happened to the truck." Autumn slipped down, rifle in hand.

"My guess is that every tire in the place is flat."

"Mine, too. See anything around that smoke cloud?"

"The chopper has to be down, but I can't get a look. If we've got rustlers on the ground, we might have a chance of rounding them up." He pocketed his binoculars in his bulky winter coat. "I need a horse."

"Take Aggie, I can get Bella out of the field." She slid to the ground. "How many men are there?"

"Won't know for sure until we ferret 'em out, but we do know they're armed and likely to be cranky at us for grounding them." Justin bounded onto the mare, talking quietly to her. Aggie wasn't used to being ridden by anyone else, and she cast a long, pleading look before Justin signaled her with his knees and pressed her forward down the crumbling slope.

Autumn stuck two fingers in her mouth and whistled. In the meadow, a few colts moved closer to their mamas, and mares lifted their heads nervously. Only one horse broke from the herd and paraded head up, mane and tail flying.

Bella. Autumn slipped and slid down to the valley floor, startling small creatures and dodging a stray bat. When she reached her girl, she noticed that there was foam on her withers and her sides were heaving.

"Did that helicopter bother you, too?" Autumn rubbed the mare's nose. "Did you think you were missing out on the fun?"

A loving nicker, and Bella pressed her face against Autumn's stomach, leaning in. Sweet. She ran her fingers through her old girl's forelock like always and laid her cheek against the hard plane of horsey forehead. Just for a moment. A greeting between old friends.

"I missed you, too, girl." She broke away, rifle still in hand. "Are you ready to ride?"

In perfect understanding, her friend whinnied, head up, tail flicking. They were a team. They'd always been the best team. She grabbed a fist of mane and swung up, Bella already moving. Without a single lead, the mare wheeled in the direction where Justin and Aggie had disappeared and took off, confident, racing the wind.

Fencing was down. It was hard from this distance to tell if it had been cut or torn down by running cattle. The cows could be hurt, and she didn't have her pack on her. She flipped open her cell, but still no service. When they reached the hard path along the fence line, she caught sight of Aggie and Justin trying to gather the nervous animals.

"Helicopter!" Justin called out, pointing to the south. Looked like it was approaching the ranch house. The bird was white and well lit, the county's south-boundary sheriff responding.

Finally. Relief flitted through her. At least they wouldn't be stuck with an inexperienced city sheriff in this dangerous situation. Ford Sherman might well be a good city lawman, but she couldn't picture him riding bareback in the middle of the night while sighting and shooting a rifle. Sure, he had been great in town earlier, getting Loren on the horn, and her truck towed, and interviewing anyone within earshot of the diner. But this? Probably not. A lot of men, even strong alpha men, weren't suited to it.

"These cows aren't all ours," Justin called out when she and Bella ambled closer. "I see Parnell's brand and someone else's."

"Why am I not surprised?" This was premeditated, well planned, and theirs wasn't the only ranch hit. Good thing Dad had taken down the chopper. "Are we safe here?"

"Don't know. Let's get the cattle behind a working fence and worry about it later." Justin flanked the herd on one side, leaving her the other.

"C'mon, girl." She could feel Bella eager to go, and they took the near side, gathering the herd toward the downed fence. They made short work of it, moving together in rhythm, familiar and at ease. When she spotted three Parnell steers trying to break free, she brushed her heels against Bella's side and they neatly drove the animals back to the herd. A job well done. Justin dismounted and worked the downed wire while she held the curious cattle in the field.

"Someone cut this," Justin called over his shoulder, hauling up a fence post and ramming it back into its mooring. "They were going to drive the combined herds down the boundary road and into trucks."

"We caught them in time." She would have felt relieved, but the back of her neck tingled. They weren't alone. As if Bella felt it, too, the mare stiffened. Her head went up and her ears swiveled as she scented the wind. The horse was telling her someone was out there. Autumn hefted her rifle, safety off. She sighted north, searching the rolling fields through her scope. "Justin? We've got company."

"I hope it's not the rustlers. We are seriously outgunned." Justin tightened a wire, raised his rifle and peered through his scope. It took him a beat to survey his side of the ridge. "It's Dad and some stranger."

"What stranger?" Alarm settled into the pit of her stomach. She followed the rise of the ridge with her rifle until she saw Dad astride Rogue clear as a bell through the scope. She recognized the man following him. Ford Sherman, riding one of their horses and looking confident and as sure as any western sheriff.

Trouble was *definitely* on the way.

Chapter Four

Ford saw next to nothing in the dark except for a few feet ahead of him. What he could see disappeared in a fast drop. A looming cloud cover obscured all of the stars. He could make out a hint of the hillside cascading downward into an abyss. At the bottom of that abyss, Autumn Granger gazed up at him open-jawed. Looked like the last thing she would ever figure was to see him riding and not falling off a horse.

Half-hidden in the night and graced by shadows, she was breathtaking. He took in the sight of her bareback astride an unbridled palomino, both woman and horse luminous in the night. Autumn wore no hat, and her long unbound hair tangled in the breeze. She looked powerful and free and impossibly sweet, holding that rifle at half-mast. He wondered if she saw him as a city boy now, and pretty much hoped he'd gone up a notch in her estimation.

Gunfire spit through the air and made his mount dance. Ford kept his seat, squeezed slightly with his knees and spoke gently to calm the fine quarter horse he was riding. No stranger to gunfire, he lifted the rifle and carefully sighted and searched the dark line of the hill rising slowly to the north. He couldn't see much with the cloud cover moving in, but he had range, so he squeezed the trigger, pretty sure where the shot had originated. The Winchester kicked hard against his shoulder, but the distant spit of rock fragmenting and a faint, pained curse told him he'd hit true.

"Good shot, Sheriff," Granger told him. "You'll do."

"Glad to hear it." The echo of gunfire faded, and there was no mistaking the scatter of footsteps. Shadows slipped from behind boulders and trees heading for the fence line. "Looks like I flushed them out."

"Let's try to round 'em up. We've got some hard riding ahead, so hang on."

"Don't worry about me."

Granger led the way down the ridge, plunging into the dark like some fearless rodeo stuntman. *You can do this, cowboy.* He took a breath and tightened his grasp on the horse's mane, and off they went. It had been a long time since he'd been

on horseback, but some things a man didn't forget.
The symmetry of an animal's gait, the ripple of
muscle and the swing of a horse's walk were
unlike anything else. Without stirrups, he gripped
his knees forward and leaned back to fight gravity
on the steep slope. He didn't take his gaze from
the fleeing shadows far ahead. Autumn rode into
sight, chilling his blood. Did the woman know she
was riding straight into danger?

Something cool brushed his cheek. Snow? He
didn't have time to do more than wonder. His
horse leaped the last few feet to the valley floor
and broke into a smooth, flawless gallop. He was
trailing the others. Without a word between them,
the family circled the area like the ranchers they
were, looking to round up stray cattle. Autumn
was in the lead. She stayed left, flanking the area,
thinking to cut them off at the section property
line. He remembered the rugged dirt lane cutting
through the fields, where he'd first met Autumn.
Now it was the rustlers' means of escape.

Ignoring the faint beats of the county helicopter
and the patter of more snowflakes against his face,
he raised his rifle to scope the land. It was tricky
because of the horse's constant motion. Something
gleamed darkly ahead. He recognized the barrel
of a semiautomatic. Adrenaline spiked, clearing
his senses. Because of the lay of the land, Autumn
couldn't spot the danger, but he could. The rustler

he'd downed was prone on the ground, providing cover for his buddies, who were running as fast as they could for the tree-lined river. Ford took careful aim. *Lord, don't let me miss.*

"Autumn!" Granger's call of warning split the night.

Ford squeezed, and his shot fired in unison with Granger's. An eternity passed in a millisecond while he waited with fierce red rage beating through him. Finally the gun flew out of the rustler's hands and he toppled backward, winged. The helicopter beat more loudly, visible through the newly falling snow, lights flashing. The horse beneath him didn't shy from the distraction but reached out, eating ground, gaining altitude on the hillside. He felt rather than heard his cell ring. He hated to lower the rifle, but he fished the phone out of his pocket.

"We've spotted cattle haulers parked about two miles away. They're heading out." The south-boundary sheriff bit out the information like an order. "Visibility is falling. We'll do our best to track 'em down. Can you handle the ground pursuit?"

"Ten-four." He pocketed his phone. The horse skidded to a stop, sod flying from beneath steeled hooves. The suspect he'd hit had vanished. Granger knelt on the ground.

"I've got one set of tracks." He sounded more

than angry. Frank Granger was a big man, and he looked like the abominable snowman, flecked with white, bristling with outrage. When his daughter rode close, the fury was tempered with affection.

A close family, that was plain to see, and Ford understood. He'd grown up in one, too.

"We've got three men on foot." Ford dismounted, casting around for signs of another set of boots in the snow. "They've split up. I'll take this one."

"The sheriff and I will follow this pair." Autumn pulled a small flashlight from her coat pocket and shone it on a second set of tracks. "Dad, will you be all right alone?"

"Be careful" was Granger's only answer. Already he was riding his horse fast around a copse of cottonwoods, lost in the night and storm.

"Nice of you to ride along with me." Ford mounted up and signaled his horse with his heels.

"Least I could do. You don't know the lay of the land." As if that were her only reason, she didn't look at him while she drew her mare to an abrupt stop at the crest of the hill. "The snow is coming down fast. We're going to lose them."

"The trail's gone." The snow fell faster, feathery wisps coating the high mountain plains with an iridescent glow. He could see the gleaming bare branches of the cottonwoods, the long stretch of a pasture, a huge milling herd of cattle, which were dark splotches against the pearled rangeland. A platinum gleam of a river wound through it all. No sign of anyone else in this vast open landscape.

"They're heading for the river." Without chopper or trucks, there was no other quick escape. "This is your land. If you were him, what trail would you take?"

"This way." She plunged her horse down the black side of the slope, disappearing from his sight. The wind whipped her hair, making her appear fearless in the night. She left him with a sense of wonder as he followed her lead through the dark. Although he couldn't see her, he could sense her—the plod of a horse's hooves ahead, the faint hint of her silhouette, the curve of her shadowed arm as she cradled a rifle. She was magnificent, and his heart noticed.

Hard to deny the way his pulse sped up and slowed down at the same time. Ford swiped snowflakes off his face with his coat sleeve. When he should have been scanning for any sign of the rustlers, his gaze returned to her. Autumn rode out of the shadow of the hillside, as mighty as a Western myth, as beautiful as the snow falling.

"I see something!" Her voice vibrated with excitement. "Maybe we'll catch the varmint—"

"I see him." How he noticed anything aside from her was a total and complete mystery, but a faint black blur at the corner of his vision drew his attention. He whirled toward the suspect, pressing his knees tighter against the horse's side. The animal responded, leaping into a fast canter. He leaned low, ignored the slap of mane against his face, adrenaline spiking again. Snow closed in, falling furiously, cutting off the world and the image of a man leaping off the riverbank in a swift dive. Gone. By the time Ford reached the steep ledge, the boot prints were filling and whiteout conditions closed in. Disappointment gripped his gut, bitter and harsh. Breathing hard, he hauled his phone from his pocket, but it wouldn't connect. He checked the screen. No bars.

"The helicopter wouldn't help, anyway." Autumn slid off her horse and joined him on the bank. "That's a swift current."

"Maybe I can still catch him." He fumbled with his zipper and gave it a tug. Cool air hit him in the chest. He shivered with cold although he couldn't feel it. His senses were heightened. The gurgling rush of the swift, deep river hid sounds of a swimmer, but he wasn't ready to give up yet.

"Ford." A soft, mittened hand landed on his own. Her voice drew him and calmed the beat of adrenaline charging through him. Time slowed, the world stopped turning and, in the odd gray light of a night's snowfall, she gazed up at him with caring. "Let him go. Your life isn't worth risking over him."

"He tried to shoot at you." *He could have shot at you,* is what he didn't say. *He could have hit you, even killed you.* The words wadded in his throat like a ball of paper and refused to move. He couldn't speak for a moment, but he could pray. *Thank You, Lord, for that piece of grace.*

"I'm fine, thanks to you and Dad." Her hand remained on his in silent understanding. "That was some pretty fine shooting. You're not bad for a city boy."

"A compliment? That's a surprise."

"Don't I know it. No one is more stunned than me."

"Still think I'm not too ugly?"

"We're talking of your sheriff skills, Sherman, not your other qualities."

The sweet warmth of her alto wrapped around him like a cloak, keeping the cold at bay. For the first time in years he didn't feel alone. It was hard to tell in the storm, but he thought he saw a twinkle in her deep hazel eyes. Teasing him when she meant something more serious.

He knew teasing was easier. He avoided serious whenever he could. He'd gotten enough of it in his line of work to last him a lifetime. "You're welcome," he choked, finally able to get out the words. "Now you owe me."

"Me? I owe you?" She tossed her head, sending snowflakes flying off her silken curls, bracing her feet like a gunfighter ready to draw. "We don't know if it was your bullet that winged him or my dad's. I'm sure it wasn't yours. You aren't used to shooting off the back of a horse."

"How do you know that? Because I'm a city boy?"

"You've got skills. I want to deny it, but I can't." She drew away, reaching for her horse and leaving an imprint on his hand that cooled without her near. She hopped onto her horse, hefted her rifle into the crook of her arm and swiped at the snow clinging to her face. "I haven't heard any shots, so that must mean Dad and Justin didn't run into trouble, either."

"As long as they're safe." He braced one palm on the gelding's warm back, grabbed a handful of mane and hopped up. Snow had closed in, and all he could see of the river was a faint shadow. "I'm going to ride the riverbank for a spell. That water's cold. No one can stay in there for long."

"You're a stubborn man, aren't you?"

"I prefer to call it determined." He gritted his teeth against the cold, ignoring the vicious bite of the wind as he faced into it. "A little storm isn't going to stop me."

"Then I'd best come with you." She whirled her mount away from home, coming closer, and a ghost of a smile curved her soft lips. Had he noticed before how pretty her mouth was? It looked like summer itself, always smiling. Undaunted by the storm, she gave her mare's neck an encouraging pat. "It's been a while since Bella and I had an adventure. Besides, it's not as if I can leave you out here on your own, city boy."

"Maybe I'm not as much of a city boy as you think." It was his turn to make her wonder about him. As he pressed his horse into a fast walk, leaving her to follow, he felt her curious gaze on his back. Was she as interested in him as he was in her? It was going to be fun finding out.

Clearly, she had misjudged Sheriff Ford Sherman. Autumn could admit when she was wrong. He rode Lightning as if he belonged on the back of the dappled gray quarter horse, sitting tall and straight and in command. Although the storm and the night fought to hide him from her, she caught glimpses of him on the trail ahead of her—the straight line of his back, the cut of his profile and the dark glint of the rifle he carried.

So, what was the man's story? Did she really want to know? Judging by the kick of her pulse, maybe not. Perhaps it was better to stay in the dark, to let her curiosity about him go unanswered.

Maybe it would die a quiet death and she could bury her interest in the man right along with it. The wind changed, gusting hard against her face, and she ducked against the slap of snow. Thunder cracked overhead.

"Time to head in, Sheriff." She cupped her half-numb hands to shout into the gale. "Thunder means lightning. I don't know about you, but I'd rather not get hit by it."

"Hey, I'm up for new experiences."

She couldn't see his grin, but she could hear it. She didn't want to like him, but she did. He had a good sense of humor and an inner grit she never would have guessed at.

"I just wish we could have found them." The veil of snow parted just enough to give a glimpse of the man gazing in the direction of the rolling river, wistful, nail-tough, not wanting to give up the chase. "They couldn't have lasted in that river long. Not with ice forming along the banks. They would have to get out, and if they did they wouldn't be moving fast."

"It runs off our land and to a county road. My guess is they climbed out at the bridge and it's too late to catch them. Time to give up the chase, Sheriff." She didn't know why she reached out, but when her hand found the hard plane of his forearm the bite of the arctic cold vanished, the rush of the wind silenced and the night shadows ebbed. "It's getting too cold for Bella."

"Then we head in." He didn't move away. The moment stretched as if time itself had ceased moving forward and no snow fell. "I know it's a lost cause hunting anything in this storm, but I had to try. Now I've got only one question."

"What's that?"

"Do you know the way home? Because I don't."

"Follow me." She urged Bella around with a touch of her heel. The cold returned with knife-sharpness, and the snow stung her face as the wind beat her with a boxer's punch. Time kick-started, and she lost Ford in the sudden swirl of the storm.

"Whew. Can't believe it's getting worse." He eased up alongside her, sticking close. "Let me guess. It always snows like this here. It's something else the mayor didn't tell me when I agreed to take this job."

"I'm tempted to say yes, but that would be too cruel." They left the river bank behind and headed into the dark night. "We can get weather like this, but not often."

"I don't remember this in the local forecast."

"It wasn't. The local news comes out of Jackson, so it's not always accurate for us. This morning

Dad said a big storm was coming, so he and Justin cancelled their trip to Casper."

"Your dad's a pretty good weatherman."

"A good rancher has to be. You get to learn the way the air and winds feel before a big storm. Dad is especially good at it." Her teeth should have been chattering from the cold, but the brunt of the wind didn't hit her because Ford rode at her right side and blocked it. Had he done that on purpose? She listened to another peal of thunder. Sounded as if it was moving farther to the southeast. Good news. "So, are you going to fess up?"

"About what?"

"About where you learned to ride and shoot like that." He wasn't as good as her dad, but he was close, and not many men could say that. She didn't want to respect him, but she couldn't help it. "Aren't you going to tell me?"

"I could, but it would make a better story over dinner. Maybe Friday next week?" Although she couldn't see more than a hint of his silhouette, she knew he was smiling. She just *knew* it.

"Will you ever stop?" She was not about to fall victim to his charm.

"Not until you say yes." The thing is, he didn't sound charming in that flattering way insincere men did. Without her prior assumptions about him, he came across as an honest, solid guy. He lowered his voice a note and drew his horse closer. "Here's a warning. I can be persistent."

"Then I would be smart to keep you at arm's length, wouldn't I?" Tempting not to. Very tempting.

"Then that's a no go for Friday? I could make it Saturday night if that's better for you."

"Awfully confident, aren't you, city boy?"

"I can sense you weakening."

Strange, because she could sense it, too. Without her eyes to deceive her, she saw more of him in the dark than she'd witnessed in broad daylight. He rode bareback like a pro. He hadn't once commented on how unladylike it was to pack a Winchester and track rustlers.

Careful, Autumn, or you'll start liking him, and you know where that leads. She rubbed her hands to keep them warm. Her insulated gloves were not doing their job, which meant the temp was falling fast.

"Well? Can I pencil you in for Saturday dinner?"

"That's the night before my brother's wedding." She was surprised at the hint of regret she heard in her words, and more surprised at the twist of regret she felt.

"Wedding, huh? Do you need a date for that?"

"You *are* persistent." She was rolling on the

floor laughing, or she would be if the ground wasn't covered in wet, icy stuff. His laughter joined hers rising on the wind, and her heart lightened. Yes, it was very tempting to like the man, but did she dare?

"I'm a fair shot because I did time on SWAT and a hitch in the army out of high school." His voice changed, grew richer and deeper as if with memories both good and difficult. She would have given anything to be able to see his face, to read the emotions revealed there.

"You were in the army?" She couldn't say why that came as a surprise to her. Maybe because from the moment they'd met she had wanted to keep him at a distance.

"I learned to shoot on my granddad's property in Kentucky."

"Kentucky?" As in horses?

"He was a trainer, but he kept his own stable. It's where I learned to ride."

She had leaped to far too many conclusions. A small twist of shame spread through her, something that not even the bitter cold could dull. "And when you and your grandfather would sit and read Westerns together, it was in Kentucky?"

"Technically in his house in Kentucky."

Impossible to miss the amusement in his voice. Embarrassment flooded her. "You didn't know anything about cattle. What was I to think?"

"You were relying on what you knew of me. I'm sure Tim, the mayor, had no problem telling everyone I was from a big city."

"It caused a big ruckus at the town meeting, since all the ranchers on this end of the county showed up demanding the council hire someone sympathetic to our needs. I was in that room, so I know." She remembered how outraged several ranchers had felt when the new hire had been announced. "My dad said we ought to give you a chance, and I can see he was right. I guess I expected someone much different from you."

"And you can admit you were wrong about me?"

"It appears I'm going to have to." They crested a hill, and the wind picked up, whipping with a frenzy and driving ice through her clothes. Ford's phone rang. For a moment there she'd forgotten they weren't alone.

Chapter Five

His call done, Ford flipped his phone shut and jammed it into his pocket. He could have used some good news since he was frozen. Even his bone marrow was officially iced over. When he'd been cozied up in his old apartment near Chicago's Chinatown considering a change, being a small-town sheriff sounded nice. Friendly. Warm. Especially since he'd interviewed in September when the temperatures had hovered in the high seventies.

He was glad it would be exciting, too. Nothing like chasing cattle rustlers to liven up things. Might as well start his new career off with a bang. It had a huge perk, too. Maybe lovely Autumn Granger was looking at him with a new perspective.

"Sheriff Benton said they lost the trucks. Because of the storm, they had to put down." He hated to have to deliver the news.

"I'm thankful no one was seriously hurt this time."

He heard that catch in her voice, the grip of emotion she probably thought she could hide. "*This* time?"

"We've had rustlers before. Didn't the mayor fill you in?"

"He mentioned a little trouble now and then." Now that he was clued in on the definition of trouble in these parts, it all made sense. Trouble at the Green Ranch last spring, a few incidences of it through the year. First thing Monday morning he would be in the office going over old files. "What happened?"

"My dad." Her voice wobbled, betraying her. He didn't have to ask to know it had been a serious hit. He waited for her to clear the emotion from her throat, wanting the rest of the story.

"He was in the ICU for six weeks. For the first two we didn't know if he would live or die. I stayed at the hospital with him, and I can't tell you how terrifying it was to wait through every minute of those two weeks praying he would survive." She took a shaky breath, batted snow from her face and turned her horse crossways into the wind. "Come to think of it, I shouldn't have let him come out tonight. Next time I'll remember to hogtie him in the kitchen."

He heard a tad of humor in her words and a

daughter's love. "You wouldn't do it, and he wouldn't want you to."

"True. Plus, he's a good shot. He brought down the helicopter, so it's good I allowed him out of the house."

"Something tells me you know how to use that rifle you're carrying. You're just as good a shot."

"Sure, because my dad taught me." More warmth and way too much affection to measure. A shadow rose out of the storm—the roofline of a stable. She dismounted clumsily, a little frostbitten. "This probably doesn't come as a surprise, but I was a tomboy. I loved being outdoors with my dad riding horses, mending fences, feeding the cows."

Daddy's girl. It was easy to picture her trailing after Granger, her red hair up in pigtails, riding the fields and hills just as she'd ridden them tonight. He tried dismounting and found that his right leg didn't want to move. After some encouragement he managed to swing it over the horse's rump and land on the ground, not that he could exactly feel his feet.

"You'll thaw," she informed him breezily as she whistled and the horses followed her. Light and warmth beckoned through the fierce storm. When he closed the stable door behind them, he discovered he couldn't feel his hands as well as he'd thought. The Lord was busy in this world full of strife, but Ford really didn't want to lose a finger. It was his fault he didn't have a better pair of gloves with him. A mistake he would not make again. He peeled off his mittens and blew out a sigh of relief. Pink skin, not white.

"See? I told you." She smiled at him, looking like a piece of spun sugar, flocked in white, the sweetest thing he'd ever set eyes on. "We had another twenty minutes out there before I would have gotten concerned. Dad's and Justin's horses are here. Looks like we just missed them."

"And your other sisters?"

"Relax, everyone's accounted for." Snow shivered off her as she grabbed a pair of halters from a hook in the wall. She had to be frozen, too, although she didn't show it. The horses clearly came first as she fitted one halter to the gelding he'd been riding and patted the animal's snowy neck. "If you follow the fencing from here, it will take you to the backyard. You'll be able to see the house lights."

"And if I don't want to leave?" He swept snow off his shoulders and the front of his coat. His jeans were iced through, but he would thaw. The rustlers were long gone, and there was nothing else to do. He grabbed the currycomb from her grip before she could use it. "Do you think I'm the kind of man who leaves his chores for someone else to do?"

"I don't know what kind of man you are." Her hazel eyes twinkled with mischief.

"Then I'm not doing something right." Boy, did she have captivating eyes. A man could fall right in and keep falling. Snow melted off both him and the horse, slipping to the straw-strewn concrete. This close, he could see a faint blanket of freckles across her nose, the perfect cream of her porcelain skin and the blush of windburn on her cheeks. He breathed in the scents of snow and winter wind and fabric softener and something innocent and sweet as a candy cane.

"Don't think I'm going to succumb to your charms, whether you are a good lawman or not." She waltzed away, ducked under the gelding's neck and gently rubbed a splotch of melting ice from her mare's forelock. "I don't date."

"What do you mean, you don't date? You're single, right?"

"Don't take that tone with me."

"What tone?"

"The one that sounds so friendly and nonthreatening at the same time. I've been down this road before." She could walk the path in the dark with her eyes closed and her hands tied behind her back. "I've wised up and learned to stay off the road."

"I know what you mean. Have a few wrecks on that highway myself." He kept his attention on his currying, combing with the lay of the coat and wicking away the snow. His words had sounded light and deceptive, as if he hadn't been hurt in any of those romantic mishaps.

Revealing. She gave Bella a kiss before slipping her pink halter over her nose. Who had broken his heart, and how long ago? Was that the reason he'd moved so far from home for a new start?

She grabbed a currycomb and got to work. She shouldn't be wondering. She shouldn't be sympathizing. Most of all she shouldn't get roped in by a handsome sheriff's stories of his broken heart. Isn't that how she'd fallen before?

"So." He drew the word out, studying her with a handsome squint over the back of the horse. "We're on for the wedding?"

"I don't remember agreeing to that." She wanted to say yes. How pathetic was that? She couldn't even resist the impact of his dazzling dimples. She was tougher than that. She could outride, outshoot and outdo most of the men in the county.

"There you are!" The door swung open and her father loped in, relief stark on his face. He swept off his knit hat, knocking the snow from the wool. "You get back to the house, missy. You need to get warmed up. I've got news from Sheriff Benton I need to talk over with Ford."

So, the newcomer had earned her dad's respect. That was easy to tell because he was calling him by his first name. Autumn was all set to argue that her horse came first before any of her own needs, but Frank stole the comb from her fingers, patted her on the shoulder with reassurance and got to work brushing the rest of the snow off Bella. She didn't need to ask if he would make sure she was properly dry and warm before bedding her down. Her dad knew exactly the way Bella liked her warm oats: with a tablespoon of brown sugar and half a sliced apple.

Maybe the interruption was Heaven-sent, she realized as she backed toward the door. Over Lightning's rump, Ford watched her with a look that said he was a patient man. He wasn't done discussing a possible future date.

Well, she was persistent, too. She bundled up before she stepped outdoors, blinded by the storm. The world seemed colder, the blizzard harsher than any before as she battled it down the lazy slope of the hill. Darkness closed around her. She'd been out in blizzards before, and this one was no worse than any other.

She could hear Denny Jones's voice in the howling wind, although it really was in her memory. *No man wants a woman like you. You're impossible to love.* Years later, those words still held the power to cut her to the core. Ignoring the pain, she kept walking, determined to put as much distance as she could between Ford Sherman and herself.

Every other man she'd dated had felt the same. Why would the new sheriff be any different?

Light hazed through the darkness, diffuse and faint. With each step she took it grew larger, bolder until she stood shivering in the shelter of the porch. She stomped snow off her boots and fumbled with the doorknob. She tumbled across the threshold and into the mudroom, where she began peeling off her outerwear. Voices rang from the next room, a pot lid banged on a pot in the kitchen and the delicious scents of freshly brewed coffee and sizzling bacon made her stomach gurgle.

"Autumn! There you are." Littlest sister Addison poked her head around the corner, her strawberry-blond hair swinging. Her big blue eyes and bright smile made her adorable. "We were staring to worry. Cheyenne is all worked up thinking the new sheriff led you off a cliff or something."

"I'm here. I'm fine." She rolled her eyes. Hard not to love her sisters. "I have enough sense to come in when I get cold."

"Did you see Dad out there?" Cheyenne called from the other room. Footsteps padded closer. "I want to check his bandage. Make sure he didn't tear his stitches. You know how he is."

"He's in one of the stables hiding from you." Autumn hung up her coat. Her feet were colder than she'd first thought. She couldn't feel the floor.

She joined her sisters in the kitchen, stumbling as she went. "Dad is talking with the new sheriff."

"Did you notice he's handsome and about your age?" Cheyenne sounded far too innocent.

"And you were out there a long time alone with him." Addison's smile deepened. "A long time. Alone. With him."

As if she needed to be reminded of that. The sound of his baritone, rumbling and friendly, was recorded in her brain. The image of him astride Lightning, sighting and firing like a marksman, was etched into her memory. "We were busy tracking, and you know how hard it was snowing. We could hardly talk."

But that hadn't stopped them from having a nice conversation. Why wasn't she sharing this information with her sisters? She smiled at Rori, who stood at the stove, frying up their breakfast. The wall clock announced the time. Four-twelve in the morning. No sense going to bed since she had to be up in eighteen minutes.

Thank heavens the fire was lit and radiating delicious, welcome heat. She limped over to it and prayed Cheyenne wouldn't notice.

"I don't know," Cheyenne said as she poured a fresh cup of coffee. "If I were you and alone with a handsome man like Ford Sherman, a little snow wouldn't stop me from a friendly chat."

"The next time cattle rustlers hit, you can pull

riding duty with the sheriff." Her face felt hot and she prayed Cheyenne wouldn't notice how much she was blushing, either.

"Me? I've got my own thing going on." Cheyenne held up the steaming cup. "Two teaspoons of creamer, just the way you like it. Let me see those hands first."

"Nice and pink. See?" She took the cup and ignored the painful tingle shooting through her feet. A diversionary tactic was what she needed to get her mind and the conversation off Ford. "How is Edward? You've been awfully quiet about him."

"There's not much to tell, since we're both a tad busy." Cheyenne was in her fourth and final year of vet school.

"But you do study together, right?" Addison ambled up, nibbling on a strip of bacon. Trouble danced in her eyes. "He's cute."

"And exactly how do you know that?" Cheyenne demanded.

"I saw a picture of him. On your phone," Addison said around a bite of bacon. "Those big, gorgeous brown eyes. Wow."

"You snooped in my personal things?" Cheyenne's brows shot up. "You scrolled through my phone stuff?"

"Oops. My bad." Addy didn't look the least bit sorry. "Was I not supposed to?"

"Not supposed to? Addy! How could you?" With a huff, Cheyenne tugged so hard on Autumn's left sock, the force rocketed up her leg and coffee splashed over the brim. Cheyenne, bent on checking for bloodless toes, spoke through clenched teeth. "Tell me you didn't read my texts."

"Okay. I didn't read any of your text messages." Addy waggled her brows. "At least after the first few. How boring, all this, 'I love you, Edward,' 'I love you, Chey,' 'Meet you at the library.' Totally boring. How many of those does a girl need to read?"

"Addison! How many times have I told you to leave my stuff alone?" Cheyenne bounded to her feet. "Where's Dad? You are in such big trouble. Rori, no breakfast for her. She only gets bread crusts and day-old tea. Cold tea."

"I'll see what I can do." Rori chuckled behind the counter. She cracked eggs into a bowl. Rori's blond hair was tied back in a ponytail. Her big, bright blue eyes glinted with laughter. "I guess that means no French toast for you. Poor Addy."

"It was completely innocent!" Addison's protest was adorable. She swept a long lock of hair behind her shoulder. "I grabbed your phone by mistake. They look alike. You know they do."

"I'm not talking to you." Cheyenne's chin shot up and she stormed across the room, her stocking feet making as much sound as a herd of buffalo.

"Cheyenne! I didn't mean to hurt your feelings. I'm just saying the dude you're dating is totally gorgeous." Addison rolled her eyes. "So gorgeous."

"I can't hear you," Cheyenne called as she charged up the stairs and out of hearing range.

"She's mad at me. Maybe I shouldn't have teased her." Addy sighed. "She's lost her sense of humor when it comes to that guy."

"Most women in love do."

"I couldn't help myself. I did scroll through her phone, but it wasn't my fault because my neurons totally melted down when they saw such a handsome guy. They don't make men that handsome in real life, only in movies and in magazines. My thumb just kept hitting the scroll button."

"You were making up the part about the texts, weren't you?" Autumn sipped delicately at the steaming coffee. Strong and sweet, it might scorch her tongue but it warmed her clear through. At least she was starting to thaw.

"You know I was. Wait until she figures it out." Addy dropped into the nearby recliner. The family room was cozy, big and inviting, and the deep-cushioned couch was calling her name. If only she could force her feet to carry her away from the stove. All that wonderful heat was simply too much to forsake.

"Justin and Cheyenne and I drove the cattle

closer to the house. Did you see 'em in the field?" Addison daintily nipped off another bite of bacon.

"Are you kidding? I couldn't see a foot in front of my face out there. I'm glad the cattle are safe. The good thing about this storm is the rustlers aren't likely to come back. At least, not right away." She wondered if they had gotten away with any livestock and, if so, how many. Remembering the mix of brands, she knew it would take time to sort out.

"Dad said the new sheriff is all right." Addy swung her legs over the arm of the chair. "That's good."

"He *is* all right." Handsome. Surprising. Interesting. All of that had nothing to do with Ford Sherman's lawman skills and everything to do with the man.

He's the sheriff, Autumn. You have to think of him that way and no other.

Boots stomped on the porch, the back door opened with a bang as the wind caught it and a cold gust blew through the house. Dad's low baritone mixed in conversation with another man's. She would know that voice anywhere. It came as if in her dreams, sharp and crisp and clearer than all others. Ford Sherman strode into the room with snow dappling his dark hair and his face flushed from the cold. Not many men could hold their own alongside her dad, but Ford did. He was just as strong, just as tall, just as impressive. Integrity radiated from him.

"Stay for grub, Sherman," her dad offered as he accepted one of the full coffee cups Rori handed out. "We've got plenty, and as your nose is probably telling you, it's tasty. We've got the best cook this side of White Horse County."

Autumn held her breath. Would he stay? Would she be forced to sit across the kitchen table from him? Somewhere deep inside she wanted him to, but that was craziness. Idiotic. Inviting certain disaster. *Please say no,* she wished.

His gaze met hers across the length of the room. In the background she vaguely heard Rori's cheerful answer. "Oh, I'm not that good of a cook. You're a sweet-talker, Frank Granger."

"Sure I am," Dad quipped. "Guilty as charged. But you're about to become my daughter-in-law. I had better talk you up. You're family, girl. The wedding just makes it official."

The wedding. Ford did not blink, his gaze did not flicker, but she could hear his question as clearly as if he'd asked it with words instead of the arch of one eyebrow. She felt a tug at her heartstrings, a pull of emotions she could not give in to.

She shook her head slightly. No, she could not go out with him. She didn't mind if he was able to read her regret. There were days she wished she were someone different, too—a girl who felt at ease in a dress and heels, who was more comfortable handling a mixer than a revolver, who could stuff a turkey with more pizzazz than she could rope a running calf. But she wasn't. Ford Sherman didn't know that about her yet, and that's the way she wanted it.

Disappointment crept into his eyes. His arched brow relaxed. The corners of his mouth turned down. As if he'd taken a punch, he let out a breath. Had she hurt him? She feared she had as he straightened his shoulders, drew up his chest and gave her a shrug. No big deal, he seemed to say, but the shadow in his gaze said differently.

"No, Granger, thanks, but I'd better get to town while the roads are still passable."

"Then how about some coffee and food to go? Would that be any trouble, Rori?" Dad asked.

"Already working on it." The sounds of the oven opening, the quiet thunk of a travel mug hitting the counter, the splashing of coffee into the mug, the rustle of tinfoil and the pleasant murmur of conversation faded into the background.

Autumn stared down into her cup, inexplicably mixed up inside. She had done the right thing. Go out with Ford Sherman? That would be a mistake of gargantuan proportion. So what if she liked the guy? Ford was likeable. Denny Jones had been, too. Best not to open herself up to that again.

"I'll let you know when I know more," Ford said on his way out the door.

"I sure appreciate that, Sheriff." Dad walked him out, their voices echoing in the mudroom. A cold gust of wind hurled through the house, the door whooshed shut and Ford was gone.

She must be starting to thaw because she could feel the fire. Suddenly her shirt and jeans were burning hot, so she turned around to warm her front, glad that it served another purpose. No one in her family could notice the sadness shadowing her. No one could guess that she wished things between her and Ford could have gone another way.

Chapter Six

Cady Winslow stood at her kitchen window and watched the snow drive down like debris from a tornado. Not that she'd ever been in a tornado or seen one, but neither had she ever been in anything like this. Living in Wyoming was a definite change from her old life in Manhattan, but she was finding it exciting. Even her first blizzard. White was all she could see—white wind, white snow, white fury and the rest of the world had disappeared.

Lord, please look after anyone caught out in that storm. She thought of her neighbors down the road, elderly Mr. and Mrs. Plum, who might have a hard time coping with this weather, and wondered if they were all right. It was Saturday morning, so the carpenters and subs wouldn't be braving these treacherous conditions to work on the punch list of the beautiful old lodge she was renovating. She hoped Tim Junior, her contractor, and his workers were all safe and snug in their homes. How anyone could even drive in this storm was a mystery.

Which meant she wouldn't be going out to the Grangers today. Disappointment wrapped around her. Autumn had already called to reschedule. Cady sighed, pushed way from the windowsill and grabbed a clean ceramic mug from the top rack of the dishwasher. It was ridiculous to feel this way. She poured fresh coffee, shaking her head at herself. She was being silly. She would be just fine staying home for the day. So, she missed a riding lesson. Misty, her beautiful mare, wasn't going anywhere. She was well cared for and out of the conditions in a roomy corner stall on the Granger ranch. There was no crisis and certainly no need to be upset.

You know the real reason you're down, Cady, and it has nothing to do with a riding lesson and everything to do with Autumn's father. She crossed the kitchen, sighing at herself, the sound lonely in the small room. She was sweet on rugged Frank Granger. While he was never anything more than courteous to her, she always found herself watching for him during her riding lessons.

Completely foolish because she was too old for wishes. She'd turned fifty last May, and standing squarely in midlife, she had to face facts. Fairy-tale love only happened to the young. There wasn't a single storybook tale about a fifty-year-old Cinderella. She was a practical woman. At her age she wasn't about to turn any man's head. But did that stop her from wishing Frank would notice her?

Not a chance.

The fire in the living-room hearth snapped and popped, getting her attention. The dancing flames were amazing to watch. Wonderful, radiant heat chased away every chill from the floorboards as she padded around the couch to check on any stray embers. Nothing smoked on the area rug she'd laid down in the sitting area. The house was too quiet again. That was the thing she disliked most about being alone, so she grabbed the TV remote. Only a blank screen showed, along with a message that the receiver was searching for information. She clicked it off. The satellite dish must be completely buried.

Oh, well. Maybe she would read. The phone rang, stopping her from grabbing her book. She retraced her steps to the coffee table, scooped up the cordless and smiled, recognizing the long-distance number. An old family friend. "Hi, Adam."

"Just saw a national weather report." Dr. Adam Stone sounded the same as he had since his wife left him a few years ago, subdued and serious. Always serious. He'd had a tendency to be somber.

She knew because she'd babysat him when he was a toddler and she was fifteen. "They say you're in the middle of a blizzard."

"They are right. I can't see two feet out my windows."

"I got worried about you, so I called. You still don't regret leaving it all behind to move to Wyoming?" Leave it to Adam to phrase the question that way. He was a glass-is-half-empty kind of man.

"I can't say I haven't had my doubts. When a herd of cattle got out the other day and blocked the road to my inn and the delivery of the new heating system, I began to second-guess myself." She took her coffee cup and the phone and sank into her favorite overstuffed chair. She moved her copy of *Persuasion* onto the coffee table and draped her legs over one well-cushioned arm.

"A herd of cattle? Can't say I've ever heard of that before." Adam's voice smiled. "You sound good, Cady. You sound happy."

"I am. I'm more relaxed than I've ever been. I've made a lot of new friends. The people here are solid and kind, and the landscape—gorgeous."

"I admire you. A lot of people dream of it, plan for it one day, but they never do it. You did."

Was that a hint of wistfulness she heard in Adam's voice? She'd never heard such a thing before. He was a deeply practical cardiologist.

"How are things going with you, Adam?" Time to turn the tables. Maybe she could get him to open up this time. "How are my goddaughters?"

"The same."

His standard answer. She rolled her eyes, sipped her coffee and tried to better phrase her question. "Is it true that Jenny doesn't like her new school?"

"How do you know that?"

"Just answer the question."

"She's twelve going on twenty. She doesn't know what's good for her, but she thinks she does." That was the most Adam had revealed in his last half dozen phone calls. He really must be frustrated.

"And how are you handling it?" she asked gently.

"I scowl a lot. Ground her a lot. Little Julianna's upset by it all."

"Do you need me to come out and visit? It's a good time for me to get away. I could lend you some support. Help with the girls."

"I appreciate the offer, but you have the inn opening soon. Maybe the girls and I can come out your way."

They talked for a while longer as the snow continued to fall and her coffee cooled. She told him about her last riding lesson, he told her about the latest stray Julianna had brought home, a mean cat who hid beneath the back porch and yowled and hissed at anyone who came near, including Julianna. She told him about the paint and wallpaper she'd chosen, he told her about the practice he'd joined and the problems with it. After thirty minutes, she said goodbye with a mix of gladness and loss. Life, she'd learned, was mostly a combination of both.

Which led her mind right back to Frank Granger. She had to stop pining after the man. He wasn't interested in her. He wasn't going to be interested in her. If he was, he would have let her know by now. So far all she'd ever shared with him were brief and polite conversations. He would tip his Stetson to her if their paths crossed in town. No amount of wishing for a man, no matter how good he was, could make him want her in return.

She was a sensible woman, so she did her best to shove the images of Frank's wide shoulders and dependable handsome strength out of her mind. She grabbed her morning devotional from the corner of the coffee table. She flipped through the pages, grateful for the abundant blessings in her life, the proof of God's loving-kindness everywhere, even if her home was empty and she felt sorely alone.

Your word is a lamp to my feet and a light to my path. The treasured verse reassured her and chased away worry and loneliness. God was in charge. She no longer felt alone as she settled the book on her lap and continued to read.

Frank rammed the wire cutters into his back jeans pocket, ignored the blast of sandpaper snow against his eyes and hefted the two-hundred-pound bale off the top of the stack. The hay hit the ground and broke apart, and the last of the herd dove in, hungry in this cold weather. There. That was the last of it for now. Feed time would roll around in twelve hours, and so would the barn work.

"That's the last of it." Justin fought his way toward him through the drifts.

"It was a good idea having you and the girls drive all the cattle close to the barns." Frank was proud of his kids. They were level-headed, worked well under pressure and knew the meaning of the word commitment—well, with one exception. He thought of his second son, Tucker, who had fled this land as soon as he'd graduated high school. Still, Tucker was a good kid. Worked hard at rodeo riding and lived honestly. Frank rubbed snow from his lashes with the cuff of his coat. It was covered with ice, so it didn't do much good.

"At least we know the rustlers won't be back in this storm." Justin accompanied him the short distance to the nearest barn. The moment they stepped out of the wind shadow of the hay shed,

the blizzard hit them hard and pushed them along.
"Too bad both Kent and Parnell are at the convention. I guess we'll keep their cattle until they get back."

"Yep. We'll start separating by brand today." That was the only way to know what animals they had, whom they belonged to and if they'd lost any. He hated to think of that.

"I'll do the head count." Justin had a stubborn streak and it showed now as he hefted open the barn door. "You've been up for hours, Dad, and you've been shot."

"It's nothing." He'd been hit worse and lived to talk about it.

"Dad, you're going in. Let Cheyenne fuss over your stitches. Let Rori fix you a nice hot lunch. There's leftover Thanksgiving turkey and gravy sandwiches."

That boy, trying to use food against him. There was nothing Frank liked as much as a good meal, especially considering his former wife, Lainie, God rest her, had not been gifted in the kitchen. He had a particular weakness for Thanksgiving leftovers. He knocked the snow off his boots and barreled into the warm barn. "I'll go in when it's lunchtime."

"You'll go in now." That sugar-sweet voice was Autumn's, ringing with enough authority to scare off a mountain lion at ten paces. "And don't you worry. I just checked in with Cady, and we've postponed the lesson. You don't have to worry about avoiding her at the house."

"Didn't figure she would be coming." Maybe that was why the day seemed so dark.

The first time he'd set eyes on the woman, he'd been captivated. If beauty had a name, then it would be Cady Winslow. He didn't believe in love at first sight, but if such a thing did exist, then this would be it. Foolish, because it wasn't as if the fancy East Coast gal would take a shine to a rough and rugged man like him. He had more failures than he could count and the scars to go right along with them. It was hard pushing the sting of pain aside so his kids didn't notice. "Has the sheriff checked in yet?"

"No." She grabbed a pitchfork before he could reach it. She was pretty as a picture bundled up against the cold.

When he looked at her he still saw the pig-tailed little cowgirl trailing after him in the fields. Always determined to do everything her big brother could. Always wanted to help out her dad on the range. Affection filled him. It was a special thing to have a daughter, and he had three of them. He was a deeply blessed man. He shouldn't be wanting more blessings to fill his life.

"I'm not sure the phone is still working." She

laid the pitchfork over her shoulder and ambled away. "We're lucky we have electricity."

"You're right. I'd best get to work checking on the generators, getting them dusted off and set to go. You never know when we might need them." As if to prove his point, the lights blinked off and flashed right back on. A sign of trouble to come. "Is that the phone ringing?"

"I'll get it." She left Justin to deal with their father and trotted down the main breezeway. Horses poked their heads over their stall gates to watch as she hurried by. One cow called out with a plaintive moo. "Hi, Buttercup."

The pampered cow fell silent and threw her weight against her stall door in protest.

"Be glad you're in here out of that storm," she called out to the cow on her way into the cozy office. She snatched the receiver off its cradle. "Stowaway Ranch."

"Autumn? It's Ford."

As if she wouldn't recognize his baritone. The rhythm of his voice, the rumble of his chuckle and the honest question in his eyes all rushed back and crashed into her with tidal-wave force. Her hand shook as she settled the cordless on her shoulder. "Hi, Ford."

Had he heard the wobble in her words? The uncertain hitch in her tone?

"Just wanted to get back to your family about a

few things." He sounded in sheriff mode, emotionless, all business.

That helped. He'd finally gotten the message. She blew out a breath. Relief skidded through her in a cool, disappointed wave. Disappointed. That wasn't something she wanted to think about too much.

"The helicopter your dad shot down was stolen out of a private hangar at the Sunshine airport. The cattle haulers were stolen last week out of Utah. I'm following up on a few leads. I'll have more information when I see where they take me."

"Sounds as if you've been busy." More than she expected. A ribbon of gratitude curled through her, although she tried to stop it. Maybe it would be best if she felt nothing whatsoever for Ford. "I'll let Dad and Justin know. We all appreciate everything you've done, considering you're not on the job yet."

"I live to serve." His tone warmed as if with a smile, but a small one. He had not forgotten she had turned him down, because he abruptly changed the subject, turning right back to the business at hand. "I'll be in touch when I have more to report. I got ahold of Loren about replacing your fleet's tires. He said he would call you when he gets a chance. He's busy on a few calls right now."

"Thank you, Ford." There was nothing more to say. Silence settled between them. Uncomfortable, thick silence that made her want to slam down the phone to stop it. He must have been just as uneasy, because he cleared his throat.

"Well, that's all. Take care, Autumn." His words were strained.

"You, too." So were hers. She couldn't bring herself to say his name one more time. "Goodbye."

She hung up, feeling miserable without a single good explanation as to why. Men. Who needed them? Not her, that's for sure. No, she was just fine without a man in her life. Perfectly fine. She grabbed a cup from the cupboard and headed straight toward the coffeemaker on the counter.

"What did he find out?" Justin strolled over, winding his scarf around his throat, ready to help Dad prep the generators.

"You talk to him next time." She poured a cup, head pounding. "Okay?"

"Sure thing." Justin pulled on insulated gloves, concentration wrinkling his forehead. He nodded as realization sunk in. "Not going well with the new sheriff?"

"It's not that." She shrugged her shoulder as if she didn't care. She didn't. She would make sure of it even if it might take some effort. "I'm not interested in this sheriff or any sheriff. Got it?"

"I do." Understanding deepened his blue eyes.

He was a good big brother, caring and always there for her. "I'm sorry he's not the one."

"There isn't one." She'd given up all hope of that. She used to be more of an optimist when it came to men. Denny Jones had left his mark, and she hadn't wanted to trust anyone since.

"For the record," Justin called on his way out the door, "Ford Sherman seemed to be a mighty good horseman. Not many men can keep up with you, little sister. You ought to give him a chance."

"No way. No chances. I'm afraid you're stuck riding the range with me forever, big brother."

"I'm good with that, but—"

"No buts." Did he have to argue everything? Ever since Rori had come back into his life and accepted his diamond ring, Justin had lost his surly grumpiness. She loved that he cared for her and wanted her to be happy, but romance hadn't exactly worked out for her. The last decade without a date was proof of that. "Just go help Dad."

The lights blinked again and went out.

"Yep, I think I will," Justin said as he yanked open the door. Gray daylight spilled in right along with tons of snow. Snow she would sweep up later. A few of the horses startled, and a plaintive moo rang out. Buttercup, wanting attention.

Autumn grabbed her cup and a handful of molasses treats from the nearby bag and hiked down the breezeway. Enough light filtered in through the windows so that she could see her way to the cow's stall. The beautiful black-and-white Hereford simply lowered her head in another mournful moo. Big brown eyes gazed up at her through long, curly lashes.

"Buttercup, no one has forgotten you." Autumn held out the treats, and they disappeared from her palm with a swipe of the bovine's tongue. Buttercup's jowls worked as she chewed the goodies with great satisfaction. Autumn rubbed her poll. "Are you better now?"

Buttercup nodded as if to say, "Much!"

"I see you are all comfy for the night." She inched over to rub the heifer's ear. "Not every cow in the county has a stall like yours."

As if to say, "I know," Buttercup nodded her head and checked out Autumn's mitten. Deciding she liked the bright blue color, she tried to pull it off by the ribbing.

"Funny girl." She kept her glove and rubbed the cow's nose. "You behave, if that's possible."

Buttercup seemed amused by this as Autumn pulled on her mitten and grabbed her coffee. The lights would be back on soon, and she had horses to train. If she had a single thought of Ford Sherman, then she did her best to ignore it. She grabbed a long line and headed down the aisle.

Ford had never seen drifted snow quite like this—and having lived twelve years in Chicago, that was saying something. Lake-effect snow could be tough, but a Wyoming blizzard was, too. This was the second stranded motorist call he'd responded to, and he prayed it would be the last.

The local radio station had lost power a while back, and so there was nothing to hold his attention as he plowed down the county road in the thin morning light. His thoughts rolled around to Autumn's call and the apologetic rejection she'd thrown at him in her family's kitchen. A silent rejection, no less. He didn't think it was possible that a wordless rejection could hurt as much as a vocal one.

She really wasn't interested in him. That much was clear. He should have known. When Jemma had left him, she'd been pretty clear that he wasn't much of a catch. Maybe that was Autumn's opinion, too.

He ignored the pinch of pain—why did it hurt, anyway?—and squinted through the downfall at what he hoped was the road. He hadn't hit a ditch or a guardrail yet, so he kept going. There was nothing ahead but shadowed white on the ground, in the air and in the sky. The windshield wipers squeaked as they fought to keep up with the dizzying accumulation. No sign of a stranded motorist anywhere. Just snow like a curtain between him and the world. Cold crept through on all sides, and he flipped up the heat.

Lord, please, just a little help here. He reached out in prayer. He needed guidance because he could not see. Had he gone too far, or not far enough? Was he even on the right road? This was like life, traveling the path in front of him one step at a time, never able to see far ahead. It was trust and it was faith, so he kept on going.

Finally a pinprick of red glowed through the endless white. The flash of an emergency light. Relieved, he angled toward that faint glow. As he crept along it grew brighter until he could make out the faint shadow of an SUV.

He turned on the strobes and bundled up. He couldn't say why thoughts of Autumn trailed him as he faced the bitter cold. The storm hit him hard as he waded up to the driver's side door, where a woman pale with worry rolled down her window.

"It's my son. He's not breathing right, and he's bluish. We're on our way to the emergency room," she said in a rush, fighting panic, that was plain to see, struggling to hold it together for her boy in the backseat.

Ford glanced in at the little guy, who was swathed in several blankets on the backseat. His breathing was raspy and shallow. She was right. The boy's color wasn't good. The closest emergency room was forty minutes away in good weather.

"Looks to me like your car is high centered." At least she had known to back up when she'd hit the snowdrift. He knelt to make sure she hadn't damaged the oil pan. Nothing was dripping or hanging, so he called it good. "I can plow ahead of you, if you're up to driving behind me. I'll get you and your boy help, if I have to carry him myself."

The woman's eyes teared, and he recognized her. The waitress from the diner last night. Her name was Sierra, and she had been one of the many townsfolk who had rushed out of the diner to inspect Autumn's slashed tires. She swiped her cheeks with her mittens. "I can't tell you what it means that you answered my call. Thank you, Sheriff."

"Please, call me Ford." A veil of snow swirled against his cheek. It felt like a sign from Heaven, that this was right where he should be.

Chapter Seven

"Fine, Mayor. I'll get right on it. I've had a hectic couple of days." Ford kept both hands on the wheel as he braved what passed for a snowplowed road. Now that the blizzard was long past, white glittered everywhere in the cheerful sunshine. Bits of snow slumped over the tops of fence posts, slung off telephone lines and frosted the hillsides. His Jeep's tires struggled for traction on the compact snow and ice as he turned a wide, lazy corner and drove along the shady side of the hill.

"I appreciate all you're doing for this town." Tim Wisener was a perfect small-town mayor— friendly and good at talking your ear off. "I'm sure we can get you some compensation for all this time you've put in. You just put it all on your time card when your start day officially rolls around."

"Okay." Ford spotted the Grangers' mailbox and

took his foot off the gas, praying that sheet of ice wasn't as mean as it looked. Two days had passed since the storm blew itself out, but the county sand truck hadn't seen fit to swing this way yet. He waited for the speedometer to tick down before downshifting.

"And I'll give Jonah over at the paper a heads-up," Tim continued, safe and warm over at his digs at the city building at the center of town. "He's holding space on the front page for this story. Above the fold, he said. Folks ought to know what we're up against."

"I'll look forward to his call." Ford turned the wheel, watching for the sensation of a slide, and corrected when he felt one. The tires crunched along the snowy driveway. Looked like Granger had done a decent job plowing—no surprise there. "Look, Tim, I've got to go."

"One more thing. It was decent of you to take Sierra Baker and her boy all the way to Sunshine the other day. I heard from Betty Baker, and I guess it was just an asthma attack."

It hadn't looked like an asthma attack to him, and he'd seen more than a few of them. Over his years as a cop, he'd witnessed a bit of everything. But he wasn't one to second-guess a doctor's diagnosis, and since the Granger home was in sight he didn't want to extend the conversation. "I've got to go, Tim. We'll talk later."

"Tell Frank howdy from me, I—"

"Will do." He disconnected and prayed Tim wouldn't redial him.

The stately two-story house appeared very different in the daylight. With a thick coat of snow draping the long, graceful lines of the top story, it could have been a picture on a Christmas card. A wreath with a bright red bow decorated the front door, and the warm glow of sunshine laid an inviting path up shoveled steps. A shadowed movement in one of the big front windows told him that Granger had been waiting for him, but when the door swung open, a tall, willowy blonde gazed out at him with surprise.

"You look disappointed it's only me." He climbed out of the rig, boots crunching in the snow.

"No, I was expecting someone else. But come in out of this cold. I've got a pot of coffee freshly brewed. If you would rather have tea, it will only take me a minute."

He recognized her as the same young woman from the kitchen the other morning, the one who had packed him a mighty fine breakfast. Rori smiled in welcome as she wrapped her cardigan sweater more tightly around her. She had to be cold, even standing in the doorway. He shut his door, keys in hand, and plodded onto the porch. "Coffee would be fine. Is Frank home?"

"Don't you mean Autumn?" She didn't seem fooled as she backed into the house to make way for him. "She's in the arena working some of her horses. It's real interesting to watch. You might want to wander out there. Don't worry about your boots. A little snow won't hurt them."

"No, but it will puddle on the floor." Which was handworked and gleamed like a polished penny.

"It won't be the first of the day." Rori threaded her way through a large, sun-filled living room with a grand piano in one corner and a wide-screen TV in another. A big, comfortable sectional sofa and chairs centered the room, which had a stunning view of the Grand Tetons. "Folks usually come up to the back door around here. You might want to try that next time. I thought you might be the woman who answered my ad in the Sunshine newspaper. Justin and I are going to be gone two weeks for our honeymoon, and someone is going to have to take over feeding Frank and the cowhands."

"Cowhands?" Just how big was this operation? He ambled into the kitchen and saw what the blizzard and the night had hidden from him the last time he'd been here. Vast fenced fields stretched as far as the eye could see, rolling uphill and outward toward the horizon. He counted a barn, four horse stables, several huge hay sheds and an impressive covered dome, which must be the arena. A huge black mass marred the snow in the field behind the barn—what had to be a thousand head of cattle.

"We hired ten ranch hands. There's more work in a day than Frank, Justin and Autumn can do alone." Rori glided over to the counter and pulled a travel mug from the top rack of the dishwasher. "With Cheyenne and Addison back at school, this house sure seems empty."

"Back at school?"

"University of Washington for Addison, Washington State University for Cheyenne. They were able to catch flights out on Monday morning." She poured steaming, fragrant coffee into the mug. "Do you want sugar?"

"I like it sweet."

"Me, too." She added a couple of spoonfuls of sugar and gave a stir. "You seem like a good guy, Sheriff Sherman. Frank made it his business to know who the town was hiring to protect them this time around. You got his nod of approval, so that says something about you."

"I'm afraid to ask what," he quipped.

"Good things." She popped the top onto the travel cup and handed it to him. "Be careful when you take this into the barn."

"Afraid I'll spill? I can walk and drink at the same time."

"I'm more afraid of the livestock helping themselves. Consider that fair warning." Mischief twinkled in her eyes as she abandoned the taco fillings in various stages of preparation spread out over the counter. She strolled around to face him. "Autumn is one of my closest friends."

"Is that right?" He took of sip of coffee, which was hot enough to warm him straight through.

"We went to school together. I know her pretty well, and I think she likes you."

"Me?" Hardly. He couldn't forget the way she'd quietly and easily rejected him. She'd met his every attempt with a rebuff. It wouldn't be so bad if he didn't genuinely like her. Smitten, as his granddad would have called it.

"She's not about to admit it, but I think you've got a chance. Just hang in there." Rori tilted her head as if to listen for something. "I think Mrs. Gunderson is here."

"I can find my way." The coffee warmed his hand as he headed out the back door and ambled across the porch. Rori's words seemed to follow him, a note of encouragement he wished were true.

A chance with Autumn? Not likely. He couldn't picture it. He plodded down the steps and across the snowy lawn, shaking his head. All he could imagine was Autumn on her horse, the sun at her back, turning him down. Autumn in the diner playing down her experience of meeting him.

Autumn at the fireplace with an apologetic "no" in her eyes.

That looked like no chance at all to him.

Stunning. That was the only way to describe the sensation as he trudged across the lawn and up the plowed roadway between the fence lines. Crisp blue sky, open land larger than life all around him. He could have been a cowboy in one of the Westerns he loved so much. A very cold cowboy. He zipped his coat as high as it would go and made a mental note to find his good winter scarf among the dozens of cardboard boxes he had yet to unpack. The moving truck had arrived to dump his stuff into the living room. Talk about a mess. Good thing his brother was coming out in a few days to help him settle in. Shay would like Wyoming, too.

Horses ran up to him to greet him on the right side of the fence. Beautiful creatures with intelligent eyes and remarkable conformation. Nickers rose on the air, hooves crunched on the snow, and misty clouds of breath rose up as a handful of mares spotted his bright blue metallic cup and whinnied their interest.

"Sorry, ladies." They chased him along the fence line, determined not to give up. A few cows on the left-hand field raced up to their fence and did the same. The mooing and whinnying made enough noise to bring someone out of the barn.

"Ford, I was just about to call you." Frank Granger clapped him on the shoulder. "Thanks for giving Loren a heads-up. We've got all the tires replaced."

"Glad to hear it." He stepped into the shelter of the barn. The scent of horse, hay and sweet alfalfa greeted him with memories, winging him back in time. Reminding him of walking side by side with his grandfather down an aisle of stalls, horses stretching their necks to see what was going on. Hooves stomped, nickers rang out, bright brown eyes watched with curiosity. Ford couldn't resist reaching out and stroking one or two of those velvety noses.

"The county crime unit will give you a call. Someone should be coming by tomorrow." He wished he had better news for the Grangers. Turning his mind to the present, not the past, he spotted Autumn at the far end of the aisle. While she was tightening a horse's cinch, a palomino mare playfully stole the knit cap off her head.

"Hey!" Autumn's laughter jingled with merriment. "Give that back, Misty."

The mare raised the cap as high as she could stretch, shaking it like a child playing keep-away. Autumn wrapped her arms around the horse and gave her a hug. "You are trouble, girl. I'm going to warn Cady to watch out."

The mare responded with an affectionate nicker

at the sound of the name, and her gentle chocolate eyes searched the barn as if looking for the woman.

"We had best skedaddle," Frank said, taking a left where two aisles intersected. "Autumn's got a riding lesson soon. Don't want to be in the way."

Strange, how fast the man moved when the barn door slid open behind them. Ford glanced over his shoulder to see a middle-aged woman in an ivory parka. A cloud of brown curls peeked out from beneath her fuzzy knit hat. The polite thing would be to meet the lady, but Frank was already an aisle away and walking fast. Ford had to jog to catch up with him.

"I doubt they'll find anything at the crash site." Frank shrugged one shoulder, practical as he stopped to rub a bay gelding's nose. "These jokers are professionals. They won't leave behind any evidence."

"True, but we've got to try. These jokers, as you put it, knew you and Justin and some of your neighbors were supposed to be out of town. They disabled every vehicle on the ranch. The neighboring ranches, the Parnells' and the Kents', reported the same thing." It was well planned and well executed. "If you hadn't shot them down, they would have gotten away with a fortune in cattle."

"And we would have taken a hard loss. I appreciate you taking this so seriously." Frank turned grim. "You think it's someone in the area? Someone local?"

"It did occur to me." But not necessarily. "It wouldn't be hard to figure most ranchers in these parts would be heading to the convention."

"At least they didn't get away with our cattle. The Good Lord was watching out for us." Frank paused as the woman walked past, an aisle away. His gaze sharpened, his posture straightened and his jaw tensed.

"Cady!" Autumn stepped into sight and wrapped the older woman in a quick hug.

Now it was his turn to forget all about the cattle, for his gaze to sharpen and his spine to straighten. He prayed Autumn wouldn't spot him gaping at her like he'd been lightning-struck. *Way to hide your feelings, Ford.*

He would have turned his back, but he couldn't force his attention from her. The sunlight from the roof windows found her, blessing her, and he'd never seen a more lovely sight than Autumn Granger with her hat askew. His heart lurched. It would be pointless to keep falling for her. If only he could figure out how to stop.

Autumn kicked off her boots in the mudroom, shrugged off her outerwear and hung up everything. She'd stayed out too long, and she was half-numb again. The crackling of the fire was music to her ears. She darted through the doorway in her socks, heading straight to the teapot Rori had left steeping on the counter. It was nice to have a little time to herself to warm up, maybe indulge in a few chocolate-chip cookies before she headed to town. Rori had made appointments for all her bridesmaids at the Glam-a-rama. The local beauty shop made up in character and fun for what it lacked in sophistication.

A little girl time sounded like just what she needed. A manicure, a pedicure and highlights done alongside some of her best friends. Autumn yanked the cozy off the teapot and yelped when she saw a dark figure out of the corner of her eye.

"Hey, girl." Her father looked up from his laptop. He'd been so quiet she hadn't noticed he was there. "I was about ready to call you. Rori made me promise to have you out of here by three o'clock on the dot."

"When have I ever gotten out of here on the dot?" A call would come in from the barn, something would be wrong, an animal would be sick, and she would be waylaid. It was inevitable. She rolled her eyes, plucked the teapot off the tray and poured a steamy cup of peppermint tea. Soothing. Just what she needed.

"I invited Ford to the wedding on Saturday." He watched her reaction carefully as he tapped at a few keys. "I figured you wouldn't mind, with him being the new man to town and all."

"All right, what have you heard?" She set the teapot onto the counter with a clunk and scowled at him. "What rumors have you been listening to?"

"None worth repeating."

"You went to the feed store this morning and stopped by the diner for a cup of coffee." She could certainly guess what her father had heard. No doubt the story about the duct tape had gotten around. Folks had sharp ears in these parts, and they knew how to eavesdrop. "Forget whatever you heard."

"Fine. I can do that." His grin didn't dim. Nothing thwarted Dad when he got an idea in his head. He glanced at his spiral notebook and hit a few more keys on the keyboard. "That's not why I invited the sheriff. Figured he's done a good job for us, so I would return the favor. I can introduce him around. He's single. No doubt he wouldn't mind meeting the available young ladies in this town."

"Jealousy isn't going to work." She carried her cup to the table. "Go ahead. Let someone else have him."

"Now, why would you say that? I know you, little girl. You go after what you want. You don't stand on the sidelines."

"I haven't been a little girl in over twenty years." She stole a cookie from the plate. "And as for the sidelines, I've found out sometimes it's safer there."

"Sure, it's safer, but you miss out." The grin faded away, leaving concern in its place. "You don't want to realize one day you were so busy protecting your heart that you forgot to live. Life's risky, and love is no different."

"Love? Isn't it a little early to use that word? What about you? I noticed you disappeared about the time Cady showed up and reappeared about the time she left."

"Cady's a nice lady, so why would I avoid her?" A faint blush belied his easygoing manner.

"Maybe because, oh, you like her?" She spun on her heels, heading toward the hearth. The toasty fire dancing in the grate was calling to her.

"Sure, I like her. I like everybody." Dad still wasn't about to admit what the rest of them had figured out. He was sweet on Cady Winslow. So why wasn't he making a move?

"You know that's not what I meant." She had no sooner reached the radiant warmth of the fireplace when the phone rang. It was Justin calling in from the barn. One of Kent's yearlings was down.

"I'll call the vet," Dad promised.

Autumn put down her tea and cookie, stepped into her boots and yanked on her jacket. Icy wind hit her as she barreled across the porch and up the hill. A girl's work was never done. This was the life she'd chosen and the work that had chosen her.

"Oh, poor thing." She eased down to her knees as soon as she'd found the pen Justin had gotten the heifer to. The bright yellow ear tag proclaimed her to belong to the Kent ranch. The sweet Holstein rasped, struggling to breathe. She coughed and sighed, as if she was in some pain.

"You're going to be just fine, little one." She held out her hands for the cow to scent her. Worry shadowed those chocolate brown eyes. It had to be hard being in a strange place with people you didn't know. She gentled her voice, putting all her comfort there just as her dad had taught her long ago. "We're going to take extra good care of you, pretty girl. What do you think of that?"

The heifer reached out and wrapped her long pink tongue around Autumn's scarf. Her teeth dug into the fringe and she tugged. When it didn't budge, she tugged harder.

"That's a good girl." She stroked the soft nose and felt the animal relax. "We'll get something warm in your tummy. Would you like that?"

As if to say, "sure!", the cow gave another yank on the scarf.

"Just talked to Janice Kent." Justin strode into sight, carrying a syringe and a bucket.

"Pneumonia's been making its rounds at their place. Looks like it's our problem now."

"You mean mine and Dad's, since you will be lazing around in sunny Hawaii for the next few weeks." Not that she minded. Justin worked hard. He'd never taken a real vacation, and he deserved time alone with Rori. But a little sister had to tease. She grabbed the syringe from him. The heifer spotted the bucket, released the scarf and turned bright, interested eyes toward Justin. Her long lashes fluttered. "For me?" She seemed to be saying.

"For you, gorgeous." Justin slipped the pail between the metal rails, holding on tight. "I might get so used to lying around on a beach I might stay there."

"Don't even start with that." Autumn lifted the needle, double-checked the dosage of antibiotics and pointed it upward, getting out the last of the air. A thin stream of liquid flew from the needle's sharp tip. "Not unless you can get Tucker to take your place. I've got enough work as it is."

He winked at her and held the bucket as the heifer slurped up the warm formula inside.

"Sorry about this, girl." She sank the needle into the cow's shoulder and emptied the syringe. The animal startled, but Autumn held her and rubbed the spot to soothe the pain. "You will feel better now. I promise."

The yearling gazed up at her with hurt, vulnerable eyes.

"I've got it from here, Autumn." Her brother watched her thoughtfully, and it was hard to tell what he was thinking. "I promised Rori you would make it to the beauty shop. I'm a man of my word, so you had better get going to town."

"I've been a bridesmaid before. They aren't going to run out of highlights before I get there."

"I know, but go anyway. You didn't need to come out here. Dad is on his way."

"But there could be more animals sick. We have to at least walk though the herd—"

"Didn't you hear me?" Justin's voice gentled. "Go on. Have some fun. You never know who you might meet in town."

Great. Had Justin guessed? Her face heated. She could see the tip of her nose, as red as a strawberry. "What exactly does that mean?"

"I think the new sheriff has taken a liking to you." Justin tipped the bucket as the heifer finished off the last drops of formula. Her brother's dark blue eyes turned serious, as if he saw everything she could not say. "Just because he has the same job Denny had doesn't mean Ford is anything like him."

"I know. I'm just not interested." Mostly because it was safer not to be, not because it was the truth. A girl had to protect her heart. She climbed between the rails. It was as if she felt the brush of Heaven's touch against her cheek. Not a breath of wind stirred, and the furnace wasn't currently cycling, but she felt something she could not explain.

I'm right. I know I am, Lord. She reached out in prayer, but there was no answer, no assurance and no sign.

The only reason she hadn't been devastated like that again was because she'd been smart about the men she let close. Ford Sherman might be nice, but she didn't know him, not really and not well enough. She wasn't about to trust him. Chances were good that he was only going to let her down.

She was being smart, and there was nothing like a trip to the Glam-a-rama to lift her spirits. She gave her brother a wink, bid him goodbye and headed for the door.

Chapter Eight

The road from Wild Horse to Sunshine was busy for a Friday afternoon. Autumn had come across at least a dozen cars and an elk. The graceful animal had darted across the road in front of her, but she'd managed to miss him. She motored along the outskirts of town to the small airport smack dab in the middle of winter wheat fields. The weekend's snow had melted away to show the ground beneath. Only a few blobs of snow remained in places where the sun did not reach. The airport was busy as she pulled into the lot, found a place and hopped out into the cold.

"Hi, there, Autumn!" someone called out.

She shielded her eyes from the sun's glare and squinted over the few rows of vehicles—it wasn't a big lot. She recognized Betty Baker, her friend Terri's mom, waving at her from behind the family's sedan. "Mrs. Baker. Are you picking up someone, too?"

"My sister from California is coming for a visit. I'm so excited." Clutching her big leather purse, Mrs. Baker circled around vehicles, making her way closer. Her sensible winter boots coordinated perfectly with her winter parka. "We're having a big to-do for the holidays, since this is Terri and Tom's first Christmas as man and wife. All our family is coming for a nice long stay. You must be here picking up the girls."

"Cheyenne and Addison should be landing any minute, if they aren't waiting on me right now." She didn't see a sign of them, so maybe not. "A crisis at the ranch held me up."

"There always is one. That's why I didn't marry a rancher. Growing up on a farm was enough for me." Betty's jovial smile was contagious. "Although I had to think twice when your dad took me to the junior prom. His dimples were so impossible to resist I almost considered marrying him instead."

"And what would your poor husband have done?"

"He would have pined his life away as a sad and lonely man, so I suppose it was good that I married a shopkeeper instead of a cattleman." Betty stepped onto the curb and clutched her purse tightly, since they were about to step into a crowd.

"I heard about the troubles out at your place. How is Frank handling things?"

"Fine. Mad that anyone would try to steal our animals." A strange sensation skidded over her like a breeze in July, and it wasn't from the airport's heating system. Strange. "Dad got himself shot this time, too, although it wasn't serious."

"Sure, I heard—" Betty stopped in mid-sentence as she caught sight of someone in the single cavernous lobby that served as ticketing area, waiting area, baggage claim and security. "Why, that's Sheriff Sherman!"

So it was. The strange sensation was explained. Ford Sherman looked mighty fine—exceptional, in fact—as he turned toward them, his fine shoulders braced. He nodded in greeting to Mrs. Baker, but when his gaze found Autumn, his dimples momentarily retreated. Tension crept into his jaw.

"Betty. Miss Granger." He smiled, friendly as ever. "Guess this is the popular place to be today."

"Everyone's coming in for the wedding." The words tumbled out, surprising her by how natural she sounded, as if nothing, not one thing, had passed between them. Was that an ache in the center of her stomach? It felt strangely like regret. She decided to ignore it. "My sisters are flying in today and my brother tomorrow morning."

"Rori and Justin's wedding is the talk of the town." Ford jammed his hands into his jeans pockets. He looked totally impressive, outshining every other guy in the terminal. He didn't seem conscious of it. "Everywhere I've been this week, it's all I've heard."

"It's about time those two got their happily-ever-after," Betty explained. "They were high school sweethearts. Just the cutest pair. Rori and my Terri were good friends growing up. I'm sure Frank is happy. Am I right, Autumn?"

"He's about to burst. I think he was ready to give up hope that any of us would ever tie the knot." Autumn did her best to sound breezy, but she saw Ford's curious gaze. Was he remembering what she had told him about her no-dating practices?

"I owe you a great big thanks, Sheriff," Betty continued on. "What are you doing Sunday after church?"

"My brother will be staying with me for the weekend, ma'am. He's flying in for a visit."

"Your brother? Well, bring him along, too." Betty didn't let much in life thwart her. "I'm making a nice roast in the Crock-Pot and my homemade rolls. You haven't lived until you've tasted my rolls."

"Why, that would be very nice of you." He

shuffled his feet. "But going to any fuss isn't necessary."

"Necessary? I would say it's the least I can do." The older woman gazed up at him like he'd hung both the moon and the stars all in one night. "Autumn, do you know what this man did for my grandson?"

"Little Owen?" She shook her head, releasing rich strawberry locks that glinted like liquid silk. Her hazel eyes widened, spearing him with surprise. She apparently hadn't heard the tale.

"I was doing my job, Mrs. Baker." He felt a need to explain because he was starting to feel embarrassed. "I'm just glad I could help."

"Help? You did a bit more than that, and call me Betty. You're honorary family now." Mrs. Baker didn't relent. She turned to Autumn, spilling the story. "Sierra was trying to get Owen to the emergency room in the middle of the storm, and guess who came along, drove her all the way in to the hospital and stayed with her to make sure she and Owen got back home safe and sound. On his own time."

"What was I going to do? Leave folks to fend for themselves?" It felt nice making a difference for a change. The world had its ugly side, and he'd seen a lot of it. His weary soul felt lighter as Autumn met his gaze. His heart swung out of his chest, falling, endlessly falling.

"You did a good thing, Ford. That's what we do around here. We help each other out." She looked at him differently, as if he was no longer the last person she'd wanted to bump into at the airport. "Betty's homemade rolls are legendary. You are in for a treat."

"Oh, boy. I can't wait."

"Oh, there's my sister! Cheryl! Yoo-hoo!" Betty hurried off, her boots squeaking on the tile floor, lost in the dozen people flooding in through the glass door from the tarmac.

"Now's your chance to tell me if she's really a good cook, or if I should be prepared for the worst." He edged closer.

"She's a great cook." Was it his imagination, or did he detect a small twinkle in her beautiful hazel eyes?

"Is this like the time you told me my house would have outdoor plumbing and barnyard animals?"

"You will just have to wait and see," she quipped, but the steady light in her gaze told him differently. At least he didn't have to live in fear of Betty's cooking.

Why did he like this woman so much? She had turned him down multiple times. She had told him she didn't date. But he knew there was more to it. She used to date. That much was plain. It wasn't hard to figure out there had to be a good reason she had taken herself out of the dating pool.

"Do you know how Owen is?" she asked.

"I called Sierra to check on her." He wanted that clear. "Totally a job-related call. She said Owen was breathing easier. That's good news."

"It is, but that poor little boy hasn't been well since his father left." Autumn's concern softened her, turned her hazel irises to a deep, rich gold. Her heart-shaped face sweetened with sympathy. "Sierra has had a hard time managing everything alone. She's completely nice and gorgeous. This is the perfect opportunity for you. She might take to your charm."

He chuckled, he couldn't help it. Autumn thought he had charm. Yes! He wanted to fist-punch the air. "You think I'm a ladies' man. Is that it?"

"Aren't you? You asked me out two seconds after you met me." Her lush mouth twisted into the cutest disapproval he'd ever seen.

"Give me a break. I was overwhelmed by your beauty. Blown away by the first real cowgirl I ever laid eyes on." It was simply the truth. "I haven't asked a lady out in a long time. I can't remember how long."

"Sure, like I believe that." She shook her head at him, as if she didn't approve of a man who fibbed.

It was no fib, and he suspected she knew that, too. But he let her believe it, if it was easier for her.

She thought he had charm? That put a smile on his face and a lift to his tumbledown heart.

"My sisters!" She lit up, her brightness grand enough to blind him to everyone and everything else. "Ford, you might as well bring your brother to the wedding, too."

"Your dad already suggested that." But he liked that she'd thought to say it. "Does this mean you will save me a dance?"

"I would, but I just gave it up. No more dancing for me. Waltzing gives me hives." She flashed a smile over her shoulder as she hurried away. She sure made a pretty sight in a coat, jeans and boots, her hair swinging with her gait, her arms out to hug her sisters close.

"Hey, Ford." Shay bounded up to him, a carry-on swinging from his shoulder. "You look lost in space. What are you looking at?"

"The tall redhead." There was only silence around him and stillness within him as he watched Autumn step out of the sisterly hug and steal a book bag from the littlest Granger daughter. Every time he saw Autumn, he saw more of her. Today he saw pieces of her spirit—loving, devoted and kind.

"I'm going to marry her," he said.

"Marry her? You?" Shay's jaw dropped. "I thought you didn't believe in that stuff."

"I did, too." He'd heard before that a man knew who he was going to marry right from the start. He'd never really believed it, not until it happened to him. He could see glimpses of the future with Autumn in it. He could hear the music of her laughter. He could feel the comfort of her loving kindness. It was as if Heaven was with him again, gently guiding him. *And we know that all things work together for good to those who love God.* The verse from Romans reminded him who was leading him where he was meant to go.

Autumn gave him a smile and a little finger wave as she headed toward the door, flanked by her sisters, their conversation merry. Her voice stood out above all the rest. The places in his heart he'd thought he had lost long ago came fully alive as she strolled through the doors and away from him in the sun-swept lot.

Ford Sherman stayed in her thoughts all the way home. Not at the back of her mind, where he had been dwelling lately, but right up front where she couldn't ignore him. Where she could hardly pay attention to her sisters because he was there.

"Ooh, your phone beeped, Cheyenne." Addison strained against the seat belt as the truck chugged up the driveway. "Is it from Edward?"

"How should I know? I haven't looked at it." Cheyenne was doing her best to appear unaffected, but no one was fooled. This was her first love, and the way her eyes sparkled said more than she probably intended. "How about you? There have to be some cute guys at the U-Dub."

"Tons." Addy shrugged. "But am I interested? Not enough to let a single one of them catch me. I have a lot of guy friends, but that's it."

"Keeping your options open?" Chey teased.

"Way open. Permanently open." Addy's big blue eyes sparkled, just the way Dad's did, and no doubt there was a large group of very disappointed, besotted college men at the University of Washington. "I'm glad Rori is taking Justin off our hands, don't get me wrong, but marriage isn't for me. No one can rope me in."

"You sound way too much like Tucker." Cheyenne laughed. "And me, not too long ago."

It was good to see Cheyenne happy. She hadn't always been lucky in love. She'd never even had a boyfriend before. Cheyenne's problems were shyness and intelligence that had stymied most of the boys in high school. Autumn and her sisters had both spent a lot of weekend nights at home putting together jigsaw puzzles with their dad. Autumn still did.

"You aren't going to move away from us if things get more serious with Edward?" Addison's seat belt was the first one unbuckled as the truck rolled to a stop in front of the garage. "You are going to make him move here, aren't you?"

"We haven't discussed that exactly." Cheyenne blushed, as if she had been thinking a lot on that subject. "He wants to be an equine vet. He needs to be near horses to do that."

"Cool. We have a lot of horses here." Addy launched out of the door and landed with a two-footed thud. "Whose car is that?"

"Mrs. Gunderson's." Autumn turned off the engine and pocketed her keys. "The new housekeeper."

"Rori found someone already?" Cheyenne perked up. "That's great news. Is she a good cook?"

"I guess we'll find out. She promised to have lunch ready when we pulled in." She looked for her keys and realized she had just put them in her pocket. Showed her mind was back in the airport terminal. She shut the door and followed her sisters up the back walkway to the porch.

She had witnessed another side of Ford Sherman today, a deeper layer she hadn't guessed was there. He had gone beyond the call of duty for little Owen. Very hard not to like him more for that.

How do I get him out of my head, Lord? She took it to prayer because she was desperate.

"Autumn?" Her name brought her back to the present.

She realized she was standing in the mudroom door, coat hanging behind her on the coat tree. Mrs. Gunderson, a short, pleasantly plump, sixty-ish woman with a fringe of pretty gray curls, posed next to the table, looking at her expectantly.

"Milk or juice?" the woman asked again, a container in either hand.

"Milk." She noticed the curious glances her sisters shared, and she certainly hoped they hadn't leaped to any conclusions. No one had mentioned the new sheriff on the way home, but that didn't mean her sharp-eyed sisters hadn't noticed that she'd been talking with the drop-dead-gorgeous sheriff.

"The lasagna smells delicious, Mrs. Gunderson." She slipped into her chair. Her stomach growled. She couldn't remember any meal looking so appealing. The casserole had been prepared with care, topped with melted cheese, and the salad and homemade garlic bread could have been the highlight of a food channel show.

"Whew, that's a relief. I hope you girls enjoy." The older woman smiled self-consciously and perhaps a tad nervously. First days on the job were always so hard. She finished pouring Autumn's milk and backed away. "Your father said to tell you he and Justin already ate."

"Have you eaten?" Autumn asked as she folded her hands. She felt her sisters' interest as they watched the kindly lady blush.

"Well, no."

"Join us," Cheyenne urged. "We want to get to know you."

"Yeah," Addy seconded.

"We'll let Addy grill you instead of me," Cheyenne added.

"Oh, all right. After all, I do work for you. I have to do what you say." With a smile of pleasure, Mrs. Gunderson tapped toward the cupboards. "Let me just get a plate."

Autumn's mind kept wanting to loop back to Ford. To the man who had done more in his first week as a resident of Wild Horse than the last sheriff had managed to do in his two-year term. That said something about the man. A tiny piece of longing slipped into her heart, the old longings of a long-ago, more optimistic Autumn Granger.

A smart woman wouldn't let even the tiniest of wishes in. She did her best to push them out. She *had* to stop thinking about him. She bowed her head as Addy began the blessing.

"You live in a barn."

"Yes, but it's a small barn. A stable, really. It's trendy." Ford watched his brother scratch his head in puzzlement. He hopped out of the truck. In the shelter of the carport the timid first fall of snow didn't touch him. The cottony clouds overhead had moved in swiftly. The forecasters were calling for four inches before the night was over.

"Dude, you live in a *barn*." Shay laughed, shaking his shaggy blond hair. "Grandpop would love it."

"He would love everything about this place." Snowflakes danced and whirled as he trudged up the shoveled walkway toward the house. A fine sheen of white spread out as he unlocked the front door. There was someone Grandpop would particularly like. Why couldn't he get Autumn Granger out of his mind?

Because seeing her today had only solidified his suspicions. He wasn't going to get over her. His feelings were too deep. What did a man do when the woman he'd fallen in love with didn't feel the same? Not even close to it?

He left it to God, that's what. *Trust in the Lord with all your heart, and lean not on your own understanding. In all your ways acknowledge Him, and He shall direct your paths.*

"Bro, someone's comin'." Shay hopped onto the narrow porch and gestured toward the driveway.

His first thought turned to Autumn even as he knew it wasn't her. He recognized the old Chevy pickup ambling to a stop. The passenger window rolled down, revealing a gray-haired lady with wire-rimmed glasses and a friendly smile.

"Good afternoon, Sheriff. We just wanted to check up on you. See how you are getting along." Velma Plum leaned out her window. "Hal, go ahead and give this to him. Sheriff, I made tuna casserole for lunch, and there was simply too much. Hal and I can't eat all of that, I said to myself, and do I know someone who could use a good home cooked meal? You came to mind."

Ford left his keys in the lock and jogged the few steps to the truck. "That's mighty thoughtful of you. If it tastes as good as it smells, you've made me a very happy man."

Velma blushed. Her husband lifted the covered bowl from the bench seat and handed it to her. "As you can see, I'm always grinning ear to ear. My wife is a fine cook."

"Thanks for thinking of me. I appreciate it." He took the bowl. It was heavy and still blazing hot. Their thoughtfulness touched him. "This is the third time you've come over with something for me. You're spoiling me, Velma."

"After I heard what you did for Owen Baker," Velma said, waving off all concern, "it's the least I can do. Now, who do we have here?"

Hard to miss the pointed look she projected a few paces behind him. No doubt Shay had perked up at the mention of food and was showing off his grin to the lady. "That's my brother, Shay, but I do my best not to claim him."

"Don't blame you there. He's as handsome as you are, Sheriff. Maybe even a tad more." Velma was a kidder.

"Hey, that's what I think, too." Shay's boots tapped closer. "I'm the better-looking of the Sherman brothers. It's nice to have confirmation."

"Don't encourage him, Velma," Ford advised. It was a joke between brothers. "Where are you two headed?"

"The Glam-a-rama. Got to get my hair done for the big wedding day." Velma glittered with excitement. "I'm sending Hal out with my honey-do list."

"Might as well be useful while she's gettin' all dolled up." Hal was always in good humor. "I'm gonna have the prettiest gal in the church tomorrow."

"Hal, what about the bride?" Velma laid her hand on his, affection strengthened by a lifetime together unmistakable in her gentle eyes.

"You'll always be my bride." Hal locked his fingers with hers. "Well, good seein' ya, Sheriff."

"You drive safe and give me a call if you need anything." He stepped away as the clutch ground a little and the truck slowly eased into reverse.

"You're a good neighbor." Velma smiled at him in approval. "Nice to meet you, Shay."

With a final wave, she rolled up her window and the truck crept down the drive.

"I can see why you like it here." Shay led the way into the house. "Folks bring you food. I saw the livestock in the field next door. This is the coolest house I've ever seen. Well, one without an ocean view."

"We all can't live near the beach." And some of us don't want to. Ford closed the door, dropped his keys on the small table and carried the bowl around the edge of the counter into the kitchen space. Wintry views from every window hid the fact that there wasn't a single picture on the wall, but nothing could help soften the effect of all his personal belongings stuffed where the movers had dropped them.

"Dude, you weren't kidding." Shay dragged his fingers through his fringe of dark blond hair. He looked over the work awaiting him. "Good thing I could get away. You need help."

"More than you know." And not only about getting moved in. He grabbed a carton of milk from the fridge and two plastic forks from the bag on the counter, doing his best not to think about Autumn. When he set everything on the small kitchen table, he spotted the Plums' house across the field.

Framed by the window, it could have been a picture—the soft yellow siding muted by the snowfall, the cheerful porch and cozy dormers. He thought of the couple's sweet and enduring love. They had spent their entire lives together.

Was it a sign, or just wishful thinking? He'd never believed in forever until now. Not until Autumn Granger had smiled at him today. Now it was all he wanted.

And she did not.

Chapter Nine

"Hold still, Dad." Autumn leaned in to fuss with her father's tie. Not liking how the knot was sitting, she loosened it and tried again. Around her rang the merry voices of Rori speaking with her grandmother, the bridesmaids chatting and the minister's wife, Doris, letting everyone know it was nearly time.

"Are you done yet, girl?" Dad asked, fidgeting. He wasn't fond of monkey suits, as he called the black tux that made him look distinguished. "There's no sense fussin' over me. It's not like you can improve on me much. I'm a hopeless case."

"Yes, you are, but you're our hopeless case." She tugged the bow until it was perfect, wobbling a teeny bit on her heels. She didn't wear them often, and she kept having to fight off visions of tripping on her way down the aisle.

Think positive, she told herself. *There will be no*

tripping and no disasters of any kind, including those of the male variety. It didn't help to know that Ford was sitting on a bench somewhere in the church sanctuary and he would be watching her. Heat crept across her face at the thought.

"Good enough." Her dad gave her nose the lightest of tweaks, as he used to do when she was a little girl and he would pretend to have stolen it. Affection reflected deep in his lapis-blue eyes. "You look beautiful, princess. Any chance you can save me a dance on your card?"

"Are you kidding? You won't have time for me. The eligible women in White Horse County will be fighting over you." She picked a speck of lint off his sleeve and stepped back. "You look nice, too, Dad."

"Nah. I'm just an old cattle rancher." He flushed a bit, bashful at heart.

That was her dad. A great man and he didn't even know it. Cheyenne bolted up, her silk gown whispering as she skidded to a stop. "Dad, look at you. Addy, get over here with the camera."

"Now, don't you go taking my picture." He shook his head, holding up one hand as if to bolt for the door.

He wasn't going anywhere, because she grabbed his elbow and held him captive. "Don't make me wish I'd brought my lasso."

"Okay, I've got enough shots of the bride for

now." Addy tapped over, the most at home of any of the Granger girls in her heels. She looked adorable in the soft sage-green dress, and her big baby-blues lit up when she spotted their father. "Oh, wow. Dad. *Wow*. Group picture!"

"We need to get one of you ladies first." He wriggled out of their grips, slicker than rain rolling off a tin roof. "Give me that camera."

"Dad," Cheyenne complained. "We want one with you."

"You all are too beautiful for the likes of me." He snatched Addy's little camera from her. No one was better at escaping the center of attention than their dad. "Go on. Get together. I want a picture of my girls."

It was the love in his words that hit her hard. She shuffled into place with her sisters, winding up in the center because she was the tallest. Addy snuggled up on her left, Cheyenne on her right. They must appear like three peas in a pod with their identically styled hair and matching princess dresses. It wasn't often Dad had this opportunity.

"You three are my dream come true. My beautiful little girls, all grown up." Frank lifted the camera and squinted. Hard not to think about the kind of father he was. Always there, always loving, always good. They didn't make men like her dad these days. Maybe that was her problem. No man had really ever measured up to her dad. And if Ford Sherman came to mind, she didn't have to acknowledge it.

"Great." Dad snapped a few pictures. "Now we need one with Rori."

"First, one with you." Autumn stepped out of line to wrestle the camera from him. He didn't struggle too hard. Maybe he was more emotional than she suspected, or maybe he simply understood her without words, the way he did so often. "Aunt Carol. Will you help us out?"

"I would love to, dear." She tapped across the crowded little room, neatly dodging the chaos. She had raised three rough-and-tumble sons, so she was a pro at chaos and cameras. "Get in there, Frank. Don't be shy."

"Shy? I don't want to mess up the pretty picture." His protest fell on deaf ears.

Autumn pulled him over, and her sisters held on. They gathered around him, refusing to let him go. This would be a moment they would want to remember for all time.

"Smile, now," Aunt Carol sang. "That means you, Frank. I want to see your matching dimples. That's it. Perfect."

A few clicks and he was free to step away.

"Rori!" Addy called, shouting over the tops of heads. "We need you, Sage and Giselle, too."

"There's no time!" Doris clapped her hands.

"You must take your positions. Calling all brides-maids! Follow me. Frank, you had best go find Justin. He's probably wondering what's become of you."

"Will do." He remembered what it was like to be a groom moments before the ceremony started. "But first things first. You will have to start late, Doris, because I want a moment alone with Rori."

"Frank Granger, if you mess up my schedule, so help me." Doris might threaten, but she didn't look as if she meant it.

"It will just take a moment." He flashed her his best smile. It always seemed to work wonders. "Rori, is that all right with you?"

"Yes, Frank." The gal beamed, tears already glistening. "You aren't going to make me cry, are you? I don't want to mess up my makeup."

"Honey, you had best get used to it. It's going to be that kind of a day." While Doris clapped her hands, ushering the bridesmaids from the rooms and ordering the others back to the sanctuary, he pulled a black jeweler's box from his tux's pocket. She was really surprised, and that delighted him. A man didn't gain a daughter-in-law every day, so he intended to do this right. "This was my mother's."

"No, I couldn't." She shook her head, making her carefully styled tendrils bounce and sway. He'd known Rori since she was a little girl barely big enough to climb onto her red gelding's back and race through the fields with his girls. He looked at her and saw ponytails and freckles. Time ticked by, little girls grew up and the cycle of life started all over again.

"My mom wore this on her wedding day. Her mother-in-law had given it to her, just as her mother-in-law had done before her. Since Lainie is gone, I'll step in and carry on the tradition." He lifted the diamond tiered necklace from its black velvet bed. "This has been in my family for four generations, and now it's yours. Welcome to the family, Rori."

"Oh, it's far too valuable." Her eyes sparkled as the light hit the diamonds.

He knew it was hard for any woman to turn down so many carats, so he pressed the jewelry into her hands. "I'm no good at clasps, or I would help you with it."

"Thank you. You know how much this means to me."

"I do. It's been a long road getting here, but I promise it will be worth it. You and my boy are going to be happy."

"We are." She smiled as if that was beyond all doubt. She slipped the string of gold and glitter around her neck and secured the clasp. "I'm not just getting a husband today. I'm getting a new family, people I have loved for most of my life."

"That's how we feel about you, missy."

"That's good to hear. There's something else that makes this day special." She laid her hand gently on his sleeve. "In a few more minutes, I am going to have a dad again."

"That you are." He didn't tear up often, but wasn't ashamed to admit it was about to happen. Her parents had died when she was young. "That means a lot, girl. Now take my arm and let me escort you out of here before Doris comes back looking to take a piece out of my hide. Your grandfather is probably wondering where you are."

He did feel as if Rori was already family as he led her into the vestibule where Del lit up like Christmas morning at the sight of his granddaughter.

"What a sight you are." The elderly man blinked back a few tears. "For a moment I almost thought you were my Polly, but it couldn't be. That was more years ago than I care to count."

"I count every one of them as blessings, dear." Polly Cornell smiled at her husband. "Rori, dear, you look lovely. Addison, do you still have that camera? I want a picture with Rori."

"Oh, I love being the photographer!" Addy

broke away from her sisters in a swirl of light green silk and began directing the bride and her grandparents about where to stand.

He left them to their work and circled to the door. A burst of snow met him as he pounded onto the front steps.

"Oh!" Startled, Cady Winslow jumped back on the step, her hand flying to her throat.

One look into her big green eyes and his command of the English language flew out of his head right along with every ounce of his common sense. "Uh—" he stammered, hunting around in his brain for the right words—well, any words would do. "I didn't see you there."

As if that wasn't obvious. *Way to impress the pretty lady, Granger.*

"I was in a hurry," Cady explained, flushing a bit. "I wasn't watching where I was going."

"Me, neither." A sorry excuse, that's what he was, getting tongue-tied. It happened every time he was around her. Maybe it was her incredible beauty that intimidated him. She could have walked off a magazine advertisement with her carefully styled hair and flawless complexion. His face heated, betraying how uneasy he felt. "I'm rattled. My son's getting married in a few minutes and I'm almost as nervous as when I took the plunge."

"I'm told a touch of anxiety is normal."

When she smiled, she could make the earth stop turning. He smiled back and their gazes met. A lasso looped around his heart, holding him captive. He was in big trouble. His arm shot out and opened the door for her. "Best get in out of this cold," he advised.

He lost his breath when she swept by. He breathed in a light scent of vanilla and snowflakes as she hesitated, half in, half out of the door.

"Congratulations, Frank. I'll see you at the recep-tion."

Was that a tiny plea he read in those emerald-green depths? Or was it simply his wishful thinking? He'd give an arm for the right to be with a woman like her. Smart, beautiful, kind and did he mention classy? She moved like a ballerina with an unconscious grace that made the world fade all around her. She unbuttoned her coat and brightened as she greeted someone out of his sight.

The trouble was, she didn't brighten like that for him. When he talked with her, she was quiet and reserved and sometimes uncomfortable. He couldn't deny that he was, too.

"Dad?"

Something touched his arm, startling him. He whipped around to see his youngest son looking dapper in a black tux, the white shirt setting off his bright blue eyes and white smile. It was like looking at a carbon copy of himself twenty-five years ago. Trouble hooked upward in Tucker's grin.

"Don't even say it." Frank hung his head, leading the way down the steps quickly. He'd been caught gaping at the woman red-handed. No doubt every bit of his heart had shown on his face. That's what a man got for letting his guard down.

"So, Justin was right." Tucker trailed behind him, huffing to keep up. "I didn't believe him when he told me at Thanksgiving. But it's true, isn't it? You've got a thing for the new lodge lady."

"I don't have commitment issues the way you do." The best defense was a good offense. "I'm not going to waste my time hoping the next wedding in this family is yours."

"You're giving me hives, Dad. A wedding? Me?" Tucker loped along, carefree and easygoing. Nothing had ever troubled that boy too much. "I'm about as likely to settle down as you are to get married again."

"It's not that I don't want to." He opened the basement door and ducked out of the weather. He couldn't admit that after deciding to take a step forward with Cady and ask her out, he hadn't been able to decide for sure if that was something she would like.

"I can't leave the two of you alone for two seconds." Doris marched around a corner, shaking her head at him. "Look at you. Windblown. Covered with snow. The music is starting, the bridesmaids are queued and Justin is alone."

"Had some business to attend to." Frank brushed snow off the front of his jacket.

"Don't you go giving me excuses with that charm of yours." Doris had had his number since grade school. "Get up there now before I take a switch to you."

"Doris, you wouldn't hurt a fly."

"Don't tempt me." She laughed like the old friend she was. "Now scoot. Off with the likes of you."

He found Justin at the head of the stairs, glancing out at the gathering. The sanctuary was standing room only as organ music serenaded the crowd into silence.

"Are you ready, son?"

"Absolutely." His oldest boy stood straight and strong, no longer nervous. "You still have the ring?"

"What kind of dad would I be if I didn't?" He patted his jacket pocket, where he'd tucked his mother's diamond-studded wedding band.

If he caught sight of a tall, willowy woman in a navy dress squeezing into a place against the far wall, Frank ignored the pang of wishing that dug deep into his chest. As a rancher he had learned all things had a season. Maybe at fifty-three years of age all his chances had passed him by.

"Someone wise told me something I'll never forget." Justin lowered his voice and leaned in, and the serious affection carved into his features made it clear he understood. "Life is a demanding trail ride. The pain and the struggle are part of the experience."

"It's come to this. My son giving me advice." Frank shook his head, rolled his eyes and wished the boy wasn't spot on. "I don't need advice."

"You need something, Dad, and I'm going to give it to you." Justin winked. He looked good, all grown up, a man through and through. "Sometimes you get knocked to the ground, but you've got to get up. You've got to finish the ride. Maybe the reward you find there is worth the pain and the risk. When you get it right, that's the best life has to offer. Love is the greatest thing there is."

"I know that, son." His own words repeated back to him. Not that he didn't already know it. Love was his life. Love for his kids, love for his land and those of God's creatures he took care of. The trouble was, he didn't know if he was up for more rejection. He gave his son a one-armed hug. "Enough about me. Let's get you married, boy."

* * *

When she was a little girl, Autumn had loved playing wedding. She and her sisters had taken turns wearing a white eyelet dress of their mom's they'd raided from her closet, and the white net from one of her hats became a veil. She remembered stepping out of Mom's way-too-big high-heeled shoes as they had taken turns parading down the aisle of chairs they'd lined up in the dining room.

Even dedicated tomboys dream of being a bride one day, and in her girlhood fantasies full of white lace and roses her wedding day was a dream just like this. Surrounded by family and friends and the faces she'd known through her lifetime. The first notes of the *Moonlight* sonata lifted above the glee and laughter. Pale pink and butter-yellow roses were everywhere. Candles flickered on pink tapers and pastel mints adorned platters on every table. There was a giant fluffy confection of a wedding cake with a perfect bride and groom waltzing on top.

"Remember wearing Mom's dresses and heels?" Cheyenne sidled close. "I don't know why I remembered that."

"It's the flowers." Addy bopped up, her eyes never leaving the lone couple in the middle of the dance area. "We used to pick roses from Gran's garden."

The memories swept back of the three of them parading through the walled garden next to the house and choosing the prettiest blossoms for their bridal bouquets. All shades of pink roses and the brightest of yellow. In memory, she saw the little girls they used to be running with fists full of fragrant blooms into the kitchen, shouting for their mom to see. Those had been better times, before Mom's unhappiness had torn their family apart. Illness had taken her away from them sixteen years ago, but her loss still hurt.

"Mom loved weddings." Cheyenne popped a mint into her mouth and fell silent.

They all did. They had grown up without her. The emptiness she left behind had gradually faded except for occasions like this. Autumn knew both of her sisters were thinking how much their mother would have loved today. Justin seemed transformed in his handsome black tux. Rori, in her grandmother's wedding gown, had never looked more beautiful as they circled slowly in the sweeping waltz, caught in each other's arms, lost in each other's eyes.

Love happened, she had to remember that. Somewhere along the way she had given up on the idea that happily-ever-after could ever happen for her. There had to be some stalwart and good man in the world who could love a cowgirl just the way she was, right?

Although looking around the room, she didn't see one. What she saw were her failed relationships. Romances gone bad. In high school, Troy Walters had told her she ought to take up cooking and learn that her place wasn't on the range but in the home. Andy Miller had broken up with her in ninth grade because she had run faster than he did at the Fourth of July picnic's festivities. That was just the start of it. She recognized face after face—Tim Wisener Junior, Randy Tipple, Boze Baker—all of them had rejected her after seeing how well she could run, rope, ride or shoot.

She didn't want to change those things about herself. She loved the ranch, she loved working alongside her dad and her big brother. She adored spending her days with horses and cows beneath the wide open sky, freezing in winter, crisping in summer and even hunting down rustlers in a blizzard.

But I want this, too, Lord. She could not lift her gaze from the sight of Rori. Joy that swirled around the new bride shone like light from above. Dad always said that the best thing in life was love.

Autumn sighed, wishes uplifting her. Maybe it was the dress she wore and the heels uncomfortably squishing her toes, but she felt different today. She saw again the little girl she used to be, the girl who dreamed of her wedding day and of the prince who would love her just the way she was. The lilting music stopped, the bride and groom's first dance together came to an end, and a man's comforting baritone rumbled into her thoughts.

"May I have this dance?" Ford Sherman asked and held out his hand.

Chapter Ten

Ford's heart jackhammered so hard against his ribs he feared she would see it beneath his shirt and tie.

"Dance? With you?" Autumn's rosebud mouth softened into what he feared was amusement as she looked him up and down.

He'd never been more aware of his height, his shortcomings or the fact that he'd worn the tie Shay had talked him into instead of the sedate blue one he'd picked out. She placed her hand in his. Awareness rolled through him like dawn across a night sky, bringing light where none had been before.

"I suppose I could survive it." Her breezy answer didn't fool him.

"Don't worry. I don't bite and I've had all my shots," he reassured her, so she wouldn't guess he had her figured out. There was a vulnerable cast in her golden hazel eyes and a hint of openness, as if her guard had gone down a notch.

"Whew. That's a relief," she quipped.

They shared a smile but it felt like more. The smile went deeper, past the heart and farther still. He curled his fingers around the curve of her smaller hand. Hard not to think about how right it felt there, soft as silk against his callused palm. He led her to the dance floor and pulled her into the circle of his arms.

"It's been a long time since I've danced." Her hand settled on his shoulder.

"I don't believe it." He slid into the first three-step, keeping his hand firm on her back. "A woman as awesome as you must have men lining up to dance with her."

"Didn't you look around?" She shook her head at him as if she found him lacking in intelligence, common sense or both. "No long line of men. You are the only one to ask me, and it's because you don't know any better."

"No, that's not why." He kept a respectful distance between them, but he didn't want to. "I know exactly what I was doing. Facing rejection again. Except this time you said yes. Why?"

"That's one secret I refuse to reveal." She flushed a bit, pink staining her face in the most attractive of ways. Candy-sweet, that was Autumn Granger. He'd thought her magnificent on the back of a horse, but in her elegant dress and with her hair pulled up into an artful knot at the back of her head, she looked like a storybook princess come to life—one too beautiful to be real—and she was in his arms.

"Was it because everyone was watching?" he asked.

"Hardly. I felt pity for you, Ford. Nothing but pity. No other woman would apparently have you, so I thought I would be a Good Samaritan. Do my good deed for the day."

"Decent of you."

"Well, it's my faith."

She so wasn't fooling him. Not a bit. He could see right through her motives to the sweetness beneath. It had taken a while to get her defenses to go down a little, and he had to wonder what had made her put them up so high in the first place.

"There's a flaw in your logic." He kept his voice low and intimate, moving in a little closer to whisper in her ear. "Your pity isn't necessary. I didn't ask any other woman to dance. Only you."

"Then I'm here under false pretenses." She didn't move away. Her hand on his shoulder felt a tad heavier, as if she were holding on instead of preparing to shove him away.

"Not false. I asked you because you are the only gal I know in these parts." He shuffled, trying to hide the fact that he wasn't a good dancer. "It isn't easy to be new in town."

"Please, you're hardly the shy, retiring type." She shuffled right along with him. Apparently, she wasn't the best dancer, either. "Besides, single and available men are a small group in Wild Horse. Any single woman here would be happy to dance with you."

"That's what I'm scared of. Those women looking me over. I'd rather be safe with you."

"Only because I left my .45 at home." She saw right through Mr. Suave. "I told you I don't date, and I mean it."

"I'm not talking about a date." He was a smart one trying to argue his point on a technicality. "It's a waltz, and you said it yourself. You're a Good Samaritan."

"Usually helping others isn't a decision I regret later."

"What is there to regret?" There should be a law against those dimples, and he used them dangerously. "I haven't stepped on your toes. I haven't steered you into a wall."

"Haven't you noticed I've been leading?"

"That explains why we're all the way over by the band." He didn't seem the slightest bit annoyed that she had taken charge. Only proof something was wrong with the man. Every other male who had asked her to dance at any time in her life had a big issue with her tendency to take charge. He merely smiled wider, as if he were fully aware of how those fine lines at the corners of his eyes crinkled handsomely. "Not many people can see us here. Good decision."

"What does that mean?" She really was not going to like this guy. She would keep her walls up, her defenses in place and never forget he was a smooth-talking outsider who would leave when the going got tough.

Correction. He would leave her long before that, when he realized this was who she really was. She was a cowgirl in a pretty dress. No fairy-tale wishes were going to change that one unalterable truth.

"Romantic." Ford waggled his brows. "Are you trying to tell me something, Autumn?"

"I sure am." Really. The man was shameless. She pressed the side of her foot against his, keeping him from steering them toward the crowd. "I don't want to be seen front and center dancing with the likes of you."

"Because you're starting to like me, aren't you?" He chuckled and the low, deep rumbling was the most pleasant sound she'd ever heard.

"No." Denial was safest. It was the only path she could take. "Do you know what you need?"

"I'm curious. Tell me."

"You need to find a woman who will buy the

wheelbarrow load you shovel out." She could tease, too. "I could introduce you around. I'm sure we can find someone at the wedding who will be able to tolerate you enough to dance."

"Probably we could, but do you really want another woman to suffer the way you are?"

"You're right. I would hate to spread the suffering around, but I can only take so much." Was it her imagination or was she a tad closer? Had he drawn her nearer to his chest without her noticing? She felt dizzy and a little breathless. Had he always smelled so good—like snow and wood smoke?

Don't think about it. Maybe it would be best if she didn't notice how strong his arms were and how nice it was to be lightly enfolded in them. Not many men could make her feel safe.

Don't think about that either, Autumn. Being in Ford's arms was more perilous than she thought. It took all her effort to keep him from sweeping her around the other dancers and closer to prying eyes. Everybody noticed everything in a small town. They would see her waltzing with the new sheriff.

"How is it going tracking down our rustlers?" That question ought to put the rest of this conversation on the right track. Except for the fact that her feet were shuffling and his hand was firm at the small of her back she could almost pretend they weren't dancing.

"The crime guys came up with nothing. I'm still running down leads." His cheek brushed hers.

How had she gotten so close to him? The tip of her nose brushed his shirt, and she only had to turn her head to one side and inch forward to lay her head on his chest.

Good thing she was too smart to make that mistake.

"What kind of leads?" she asked.

"So far all trails run cold." He turned grim. "I checked with all the area hospitals and emergency clinics but no one came in with gunshot wounds or hypothermia. No missing persons or anyone spotted downriver."

"At least you were thorough. That's more than we could say about the last sheriff."

"I'm not done. I've been checking aerial maps and tracking down similar crimes in the state." Impressive. Manly. Capable. Not even the dim light and her own doubts could diminish him. His wide shoulder really did look like a comfortable place to lay her head.

Not that she wanted to or anything. It was simply an observation.

"I'll never forget riding with you in the blizzard." His steps stilled. The room faded. His darkened gaze held her mesmerized. "I hadn't ridden since my granddad died."

Were they dancing or standing still? She couldn't tell. She felt as if she were twirling in slow, wondrous circles, but her heels were planted solidly on the tile floor. Nothing but her heart moved.

"You gave me back something I'd lost, Autumn." His hand, the one with her fingers resting lightly on his palm, brushed away stray tendrils from her eyes. The caress of his knuckles felt tender.

Don't start caring for him. She meant to give him a shove and put distance between them, but her hands didn't obey her. She remained caught in his arms.

"You can push me away all you want. It won't change what you've done for me."

"Ford? The song is over."

"Not for me." His knuckles swiped across her cheek a second time and stayed there in a gesture of tenderness. Vaguely, he registered the quartet silencing and the couples breaking up around him. He would not take the first step away from her. He refused to be the one to let go. "Do you know what you are?"

"I'm fascinated to find out."

"You're Cinderella. You are all dressed up for the ball."

"Do I look as if I believe in fairy tales?" She

looked the part, wholly transformed in her silk gown and dainty hairdo. Her hand pushed at his shoulder, but he held his ground.

"You don't have to believe in fairy tales," he leaned close to whisper against her ear. "You are one."

He felt the vulnerable quake ripple through her like a gust of wind through chimes, and an answering one breezed through his spirit. That tiny tremble betrayed her. She was more vulnerable than she let on. Impossible to hold back the rising tide of his affection.

Just one chance, Lord. That's all I ask. He reached out in prayer as the first strain of Vivaldi began. *Just give me one chance to win her, and I'll do my best with it.*

He tightened his hold on her and drew her against his chest. She fit into his arms as if God had made her just for him.

Cady had been to a lot of weddings in her life. Between her friends, her family, her colleagues and even her clients she had attended nearly every kind of wedding possible. None of them could compare to this simple country wedding held in a small-town church. Everyone came bearing gifts and the willingness to have a good time. Folks stood around in clusters, nibbling on cake and talking about everything under the sun.

"How much more do you have to do on the lodge?" Martha sipped from a glass of pink lemonade.

"Most of the finish work is done. The decorator starts on Monday." She'd found an interior designer in Jackson, more than two hours away. "My first booking is for Valentine's Day."

"How exciting." Betty Baker dug her fork into her second slice of wedding cake. "It's such a lovely property. I can't wait to see what you've done with it."

"You should have an open house," Sandi Walters suggested as she chased cake crumbs on her dessert plate with her fork tines. "Folks around here are curious to see what you've done, and it might be a way for them to welcome you to the community."

"You never know how many referrals you will get from it," Martha pointed out, always the practical businesswoman.

"True." Cady chuckled. She hadn't thought of it, but a party sounded nice. "I'll see what I can do."

"I could help you if you need any suggestions," Sierra Baker, the young waitress from the diner, suggested. "Not for pay or anything. My mom is the president of the Ladies Aid, and she has putting on an event down to a science."

"I may take you up on that." She was about

to ask how little Owen was faring when Sandi gasped.

"Oh, be still my heart." The woman didn't seem able to breathe. Perhaps she was having a cardiac event or an asthma attack. But no one else in their little group seemed alarmed. Sandi's hand flew to her throat. "It's Frank Granger."

"Where?" Arlene Miller leaped to attention, scanning the crowd in search of him. "That man is a dream."

"You said it," Sandi agreed. "Look! He's coming around in front of the violin player."

"Oh!" Arlene sighed. "He looks good in a tux."

"He certainly does," Sandi agreed. "I can't count how many times I've batted my eyes at him and no reaction. Nothing."

"You go right ahead and give up hope, Sandi," Arlene quipped. "I'm going to be sweet on Frank until the end of time or until he gives in and marries me."

"Keep dreaming," Sandi teased good-naturedly.

It was clearly a long-standing debate between the two. Cady's face heated because she fell silent along with the other single, middle-aged women who watched Frank's progress across the room. He definitely did look fine in a tux. With those broad shoulders, muscled arms and trim waist, how could he not? Every inch of her heartstrings tugged with the sweetest and purest of wishes as he stopped to talk with the reverend's wife. Even Doris wasn't immune to his masculine charm, and she beamed up at him with clear sisterly affection.

Everyone loved Frank Granger. Cady feared she loved him, too.

"Mommy!" A little boy around six pressed against Cady's knee. His breath rasped. "Can I go outside and play? I wanna make a snowman, too."

"I'm sorry, sweetie." Unmistakable love and apology twisted Sierra's face. She was such a pretty young woman, so very much like Cady's own younger sister in many ways. The long, straight blond hair, the big gray eyes and even the way she tilted her head to the left side in sympathy. "You have to stay indoors."

"But all the other kids are." Heartbreak filled those big eyes. "Please, please, please?"

"Not this time, sweetheart." Sierra drew her arm around him. What a good mom. Anyone could see the love and worry plain on her face. "Not until you're better."

"But I'm better. Really. See." But he broke into a honking cough that was quite alarming. Just a few hacks, but all of the women in the circle exchanged worried looks.

Poor little boy. Cady wished she knew how to help.

"Mom! Look." Owen clutched his mother. "It's Tucker! Tucker the rodeo champion."

Sure enough, a strapping man who looked like a young carbon copy of his father approached the crowd. "I'm supposed to let everyone know it's almost time to send the bride and groom off. Grab your coats, because it's cold out there."

She couldn't help liking Frank's son instantly. He had the same easygoing nature and masculine assurance. Frank had raised a fine family. That said something about the man.

"Don't you look handsome, Tucker." Sandi turned motherly. "Are you home to stay this time?"

"Me? No way. Just here to endure the nuptials. Family obligation, don't you know?" He winked. "I've got the national finals this week. I'm leaving on a flight tonight."

"Where to?" Arlene asked. "Is that in Reno?"

"Las Vegas." He shrugged. "Dad was going to come see me compete, but he cancelled because of the trouble."

"The cattle rustlers." Martha tsked, shaking her head. "It's not right how they wipe out an entire ranch. Take everything. Why, how does a rancher recover from that?"

"Dad's a pretty good shot. I don't think he's

going to let it happen." Tucker turned his attention to her. "You must be Cady. Autumn has gone on and on about you. You bought one of her mares."

"Yes, and she's giving me riding lessons."

"She mentioned that, too. Well, I'd best spread the word around. See you outside."

"Say hi to your father for me," Sandi said.

"You girls are wasting your time." Martha drained her punch cup. "Frank Granger is never going to remarry, after what went on with his wife. She ruined him for other women."

Cady perked up. What had gone on with Frank and his wife?

"A city girl from Boston." Arlene leaned close to explain. "Lainie was nice enough, but she didn't have what it took to be a rancher's wife. Left him with the kids and ran off with someone from Jackson. A terrible thing."

"Then came back apologizing when she was sick," Sandi said. "What did she have? Something was wrong with her insides."

"They didn't know at first. Problems with her liver. Turned out to be cancer." Betty shook her head, true sadness layering her voice. "Frank took her back and cared for her until the end. Had to break him to do it, but he's that kind of man, and he had those kids to think about."

Oh. Her knees went weak. What courage that

must have taken. She caught sight of him talking with the minister. Frank was a rare combination of strength, goodness and compassion. The kind of man she'd always dreamed of finding.

"He's never dated once since Lainie died," Martha informed her. "Sad. I don't think he ever will."

So that was the reason his walls were up. Cady prayed that her adoration for him wasn't showing.

"Brrr, it's cold out there," Martha commented when a group of folks rushed out into the yard. "Here's your coat, Cady."

Her coat? She barely managed to thank Martha. She was hardly aware of slipping her arms into her down parka or searching for her gloves in the pockets. Frank chose that moment to saunter in, grab his jacket from a hanger and give them a polite nod.

"Ladies," he said in his rich, rumbling baritone and walked away with every last piece of her heart.

Chapter Eleven

Autumn hated to admit it, but there was nothing nicer than being nestled against Ford's shoulder. It was like an awesome dream you didn't want to end. She wanted to hold on to this moment forever, savor her ongoing dance with Ford—the texture of his jacket against her cheek, the light pressure of his chin against her forehead and the steady thump of his heart beneath her ear.

He was right. She *was* like Cinderella. Eventually the quartet would quit playing, Ford would step away and she would go back to being herself—the woman no man had asked to dance in a decade.

"Autumn?"

She felt a tap on her shoulder. Tucker. She squeezed her eyes shut, but that didn't keep the dance from ending. Ford stopped swaying, his arms released her and she lifted her cheek from his shirt. When she opened her eyes her little brother towered over her, grinning ear to ear.

It figured he would be the one to interrupt her. Tucker didn't hide his amusement as he eyed the sheriff.

"Cheyenne sent me to fetch you." He hardly looked at her as he extended his right hand to Ford. "I'm Tucker. I've heard a lot about you, Sheriff."

"Don't believe everything you hear." Ford held out his hand and they shook, looking like instant buddies. "Tucker Granger. I saw you on TV. You won the rodeo I was watching."

"In Tulsa? I got lucky." Tucker appeared pleased. "Hey, big sister, you did all right. I like this guy."

"Don't congratulate me yet. We were only dancing." If she was blushing, she hoped the shadows hid it. No way did she want Tucker to read anything into it. For one long moment she'd caught hold of a fairy tale, but it was time to let go. "My sisters are waiting."

"Then go." Ford seemed assured, as if dancing together had changed things between them.

How could she let it? Nothing had changed. That was her story and she was sticking to it. Denial was her friend while she whirled around and tapped across the empty dance area. The string quartet packed up and hardly anyone was left in the hall. The emptiness echoed around her as she wove around the edge of the cake table.

Was it her imagination or was Ford tracking her? She glanced over her shoulder, but his attention remained fixed on Tucker. The rumble of Ford's baritone followed her down the corridor, growing fainter. It couldn't be a good sign that she liked his voice more every time she heard it.

"Autumn! There you are." Cheyenne pulled her into the coatroom. "We've been waiting for you."

"Sorry." It just went to prove that dancing with Ford had been a mistake. She never should have said yes. She never should have clung to him for the sweetest, slowest waltzes in history. Storybook wishes were fiction, and when they did come true they did not happen to a girl like her. She had to forget the wonder of being held in his arms and focus on her real life and her family. "I lost track of time."

"It happens." Cheyenne thrust a coat at her. "Here. Put this on. Rori is ready to go. Addy has the wedding bouquet, and I have the you-know-whats. Come on."

She jabbed her arms into her sleeves and tottered after her sister on high heels. That's when she noticed her sister had changed into a sweater, jeans and boots. "Is Tucker taking you and Addy with him to the airport tonight?"

"I have to get back. I have a new rotation start-ing on Monday." Cheyenne skidded to a stop in the church's vestibule. "So tell me what it was like dancing with Mr. Handsome."

"Dreamy." The word was out before she could stop it. "I mean, ho-hum. A tad on the boring side."

"It sure looked that way," Addy chimed in, adorable in her UW sweatshirt and jeans with the bridal bouquet in hand. "He's like way old, at least for me, but he's just right for you."

"Glad I have your stamp of approval." Autumn rolled her eyes. "It was a dance, not a proposal."

"Autumn!" Rori swept into sight with her grand-mother on her arm and her sister trailing. She was understated elegance itself in a cable knit sweater, dark pants and boots. She shone with bliss. "I can't believe it. I'm really married to Justin. It's a dream come true."

"Real love is." That was every girl's dream. Even hers. She walked into Rori's embrace and held her for a moment. She recognized the fam-ily's diamonds around Rori's neck and smiled. They looked perfect. Sometimes the fairy tale came true. She blinked hard because her eyes were watering. "Before you drive off into the sunset, we have something for you."

"We love you, Rori," Cheyenne burst out.

"Totally," Addy agreed.

"Today is a great day for our family because you have joined it." Autumn paused and swallowed the pesky emotions knotting up in her throat.

"And we want to commemorate it with jewelry." Cheyenne shuffled close and held up the four single-link gold bracelets they had picked out together.

"Really cute jewelry." Addy completed the circle. "Charm bracelets. One for each of us."

"Oh, I love charm bracelets." Rori's hand flew to her throat. Her eyes filled. "This is brilliant."

"Whatever occasions come along, we can mark them with a new charm," Cheyenne added. "One for each of our bracelets."

Autumn chose one of the identical gold chains and held it out for Rori. A pair of tiny etched gold wedding bells hung from the first link. "We picked out the first one to symbolize your wedding and the day you became our sister."

"Oh, you guys." Rori teared up.

Autumn could hardly see to secure the clasp, but she managed it. Before they could hug, the door flew open, letting in a gust of cold and snow.

"We are freezing out here." Dad flashed his signature good-natured grin. "Get the lead out and get moving, girls."

"Yes, Dad." They all chimed together, even Rori. Just like sisters.

It all happened in a blur. Rori hugged her

grandmother and grandfather before Justin took her away in his arms. The happy couple stood on the church's front step as generations of their family and the town's families had done before. Rori closed her eyes and tossed the beautiful rose bouquet. It sailed through the air and directly into Autumn's hands.

Mortification. She stared at the bundle of flowers and ribbons and endured the applause and the laughter. Before she knew it, Rori and Justin were climbing into a hired town car and motoring away. Goodbyes and well wishes rang in the air, refusing to be dimmed by the steadily falling snow.

Please watch over them, Father. The prayer came easily, her most desired wish. *Let them find the happily-ever-after they deserve.* She resisted the urge to pray for one of her own. Some things in life would not come true no matter how much you wanted them.

"Nice catch." Ford moseyed up to her like a courting man.

A ribbon of awareness wrapped around her. She didn't want it to. She didn't want to remember the security of being held against his chest, either, but she did. She turned away, planted her high-heeled shoes carefully in the snow and ignored the cold, wet seep between her toes. "I think Rori did it on purpose."

"I know she did. I saw her do it." He tapped his

forefinger to his temple. "Not much gets past me. I'm sharper than I look."

"Well, what about those rustlers you couldn't catch?"

"Doesn't mean I won't. I'll hang in there. I'll get the job done." Invincible. That would be one way to describe him. Incredibly likable was another.

"Howdy there, Sheriff." Mr. Baker passed them on the snowy lawn, his cowboy boots crunching in the accumulation. "Good to see you've found one of the best gals in town. You move fast."

What? Her knees turned to jelly. Why would Mr. Baker say such an outrageous thing? And he winked, as if he didn't see a thing wrong with it.

"I've got good detective skills," Ford quipped in answer to Chip. Amused when he should have been horrified. "I didn't waste any time."

"I should say not." Chip chuckled as he marched along the walkway ahead of them. "Keep up the good work."

"Honestly. It was a dance." She blushed so furiously her face was hot enough to melt all the snow in the parking lot.

"To be honest, it was four separate songs." Ford stubbornly kept at her side.

Four? She had heard only two. It just went to show the man affected her. He short-circuited her common sense and scrambled her neurons until she couldn't even count. A smart woman would put as much distance as she could from the man, but she didn't want to. How smart did that make her?

Not very.

"Hi, Autumn!" Her friend Merritt popped up from behind her Ford pickup. She waved her ice scraper in greeting. "Oh, hi, Sheriff. I should have *known*."

"Known what?" Ford asked.

"Don't ask." Autumn shook her head at Merritt, hoping her friend wouldn't say anything more. Really. Merritt had nearly spilled the beans. Nothing was sacred in a small town. A person's painful past ought to be kept secret. She pulled her keys out of her coat pocket. Her beige truck was mantled with fresh snow.

"I'm curious now." He waited until she'd beeped open the locks before opening her truck door for her. Dappled by crystal snowflakes and framed by the soft gray daylight, he could have been a Western legend come to life in a stunning black suit and tie. Unaware of his impact, he curved one hand on the top of the door, emphasizing his masculine presence. "What haven't you told me?"

"Nothing. Besides, if you wait long enough someone is bound to spill it for you." She knocked the snow from her heels on the door frame. "Just wait."

"Maybe I don't want to." He gripped her elbow

with his free hand, helping her up and onto the seat. "I'm a good investigator. I can ferret out the truth. I want to hear it from you. I want you to trust me enough with your story."

"Trust." Wasn't that the key word? She hadn't trusted a man since Denny Jones had crushed her. She'd gotten hurt, her defensive walls went up and they stayed solidly in place ever since. Only one man had ever been a threat to them, and he was standing in front of her, his granite jaw set with determination and his compelling gaze poignant with caring.

"Autumn, dear." Arlene Miller circled around the front of her neighboring SUV with an ice scraper in hand. "Trusting a man is always risky. Especially an outsider. Remember what happened last time. I would make him prove himself first."

"Prove myself?" Ford's brow furrowed. Why did she find his every little gesture and every expression on his stunningly handsome face more and more fascinating?

"What happened last time?" he asked.

"Don't think you're the first charming sheriff to come to our town," Arlene added, happy to help. "I—"

"Thanks, Mrs. Miller," Autumn interrupted. The parking lot might be starting to empty, but plenty of folks were out clearing their windshields within listening range. Fantastic. Across the row Merritt turned around and offered a thumbs-up of encouragement. Even better.

"Get in." She gestured to the empty passenger seat. Ford flashed her a to-die-for grin, closed her door and powered around the front of her truck. It was the only way. She loved this town, but she didn't want to be afternoon entertainment.

Cold air rushed in with him as he plopped athletically on the seat beside her. The door whooshed shut and they were alone together, just her and the arresting sight of the man.

Maybe it would go easier if she didn't look directly at him. She could do this. She could dig up her painful mistakes and manage to frame them into words that didn't reveal how much she'd been devastated. It was going to hurt, but she was a fearless girl. She was tough. She knew how to take a hit and keep going.

There was a dull knock against one of the windows. She could see a shadowed blur on Ford's side of the truck.

"What in the world?" he asked as he hit the power button, but nothing happened because the engine wasn't on.

She turned the key one click and the window powered down to reveal a stranger with Ford's piercing eyes and a lopsided grin. "Are you going to be long?" he asked.

"I don't know." Ford shook his head, scattering shocks of dark hair. "Autumn, meet my brother Shay."

"Hi, there, pretty lady." Shay wasted no time amping up his charisma. What was it about the Sherman men that they had extra male magnetism? "Sorry to interrupt. I can see my big brother's busy, but if this is going to take a while, I need the keys to the Jeep. I could freeze in this weather."

"California winters aren't like this," Ford explained as he dug into his pocket and handed over the keys. "Don't mess with my radio."

"Dude, I can't wait without tunes. Nice to meet you, Autumn. Go easy on my bro. He's had a hard time with the ladies. A long string of rejections. It's sad. See ya."

"Is that right?" Intrigued, she tried to imagine it. Ford was handsome, polite and a hard worker. In a lot of ways he reminded her of the men in her family. "What's wrong with you that you're continuously rejected?"

"Not continuously." Ford powered up the window. "Aren't we talking about you?"

"If you don't mind, I'd rather divert the focus off me and onto you."

"I mind." That made him laugh. "We can leave my sad situation for later. What were you going to tell me?"

A series of knocks sounded against her side window. Through the snow-speckled glass she recognized her sisters. Really, couldn't a girl get any privacy? She hit the button and the window zipped down, letting in frigid air.

"Hi, Sheriff." Cheyenne greeted him without a hint of surprise.

"We just wanted to say goodbye," Addy added. "We're ready to go. Tucker's frothing at the bit to get on the road."

"Take care, Autumn." Cheyenne reached over the lip of the window glass, bracelet charm dangling.

Autumn hugged her back. "You both have safe flights. Do well on your finals."

"I'll do my best," Cheyenne promised, stepping back to make room for Addy's hug.

"And you, little sister, had best behave." Sweet to wrap an arm around the baby of the family.

"Me? I'm always good. It's you we're worried about." Addy winked as she hopped back and hiked her bag higher onto her shoulder. "You alone in there with our handsome sheriff."

"Addison, you can be quiet now." Her face heated. While her sisters dashed away giggling, she sat still, mortified. Especially when Arlene Miller looked up from the last of her ice scraping and winked.

Honestly. She wished the snow hadn't been

knocked off the window. The glass was slightly tinted but not dark enough to hide behind, at least not with Mrs. Miller's sharp eyes.

"You have to pardon my sisters. They live to torture me."

"My brother is the same way. You didn't see the thumbs-up he gave me when he walked away."

"I don't see why they are leaping to conclusions." If only she could stop blushing. "We're just talking, that's all."

"Exactly. It's about time we had a serious talk."

"Right. I can't help feeling that everyone in the parking lot knows we're in here." Hidden behind a windshield full of snow. Fogging up the windows from simply breathing. On the other hand, maybe she should turn on the engine. Her teeth started to chatter, and fog-free windows would cut down on local speculation. Let everyone clearly see they were not sharing a kiss.

She blushed harder and turned the key. The engine roared to life, and cold air hurled out of the dashboard vents. Music blared from the speakers. She silenced it and fiddled with the defroster controls to give her mind somewhere else to focus. Kissing Ford. Now where had that thought come from? She didn't like the man. She did not want to kiss him.

Fine, maybe she did. But only a little teeny-tiny bit.

"So, I'm not the first sheriff to charm you?" He leaped into the subject she would rather put off. His easygoing manner had been deceptive, she could see that now. His gaze sharpened and turned piercing.

Easy to see he had been a good vice cop. It occurred to her he was much more of a man than met the eye. That could be good or very, very bad. As it had been with Denny.

Lord, what have I gotten myself into?

"What was his name?" Ford didn't look as if he would relent. And she didn't aim to make him. She wanted to tell him the truth. He had the right to know why there was no chance they were going to get involved. That way he could redirect his efforts and find someone else.

"Dennis Jones." She twisted toward him, ignored the creak of the leather seats and unzipped her coat. "He was a homicide cop from Philadelphia. He'd put in eight years on the force and was burned out. Ready for a change, and he thought this sleepy little town might be it. Sound familiar?"

"Let me guess. The first time he set sight on you he fell hard." Ford winced.

"That's what he said." Even that small piece hurt to remember. "I was nineteen. I didn't have a lot of experience dating, and Denny was handsome and charming. I liked him."

"And you two started dating?"

"Right away. I was naive enough to be flattered by his interest. Our first date was at the diner. Afterward we walked to the drive-in, grabbed ice cream for dessert and meandered down to the river." She fingered the flowers adorning her hair and tugged out a hairpin. "He was romantic and sweet and gentlemanly. A girl's dream come true."

"So, he didn't just break your heart." He'd broken her dreams, too.

"Not at first. It took time." She was going a good job of hiding her emotions. She could have been speaking of the weather. But he'd learned to read the smaller signs, the little things that got past most people. She was leaning away from him, as if to create distance. Fiddling with the flowers she'd taken from her topknot instead of facing the truth. "The worst part was that he was sincere, at least at first."

"But?" he prompted, fearing he already knew what was coming next.

"As time went by, he figured out that you can't run from your past. Your issues come right along with you wherever you go. He hid a deeper layer of his personality that was troubled. I didn't see it in time." She pulled another pin out of her hair, and light red locks spilled over her shoulders. "He said he'd tried, but he couldn't love me. He said no man could."

"Why is that?"

"Because what kind of woman would rather ride a horse all day than to cook for her family?" She didn't look at him as she tucked the hairpins into the center console. "After he saw me at target practice and realized I was a better shot than him, he decided my place should be in the house helping my Aunt Opal in the kitchen and with the housework. There's nothing wrong with that. I wish I was wired that way, but I'm not."

"Anyone who's met you can sum that up in about two seconds flat." He sure didn't think much of this guy, but he'd seen the type. Maybe a tad controlling and secretly self-interested. He'd worked with men like that. He'd arrested men like that. No wonder she wanted nothing to do with him.

"Don't think my mom didn't try to keep me indoors. I remember the day I was tall enough to stand on my tiptoes and wrap both hands around the doorknob. Mom was busy in the kitchen, so she didn't hear me let myself out onto the porch." The shields fell away and emotion lit her up—love for the memory she relived. "I was free. I can still recall that feeling of glee and triumph."

That wasn't hard to picture at all. No doubt she'd

been an adorable toddler with big eyes, reddish curls and sweetness.

"I was going to find my daddy. My little feet carried me down the steps, across the yard and up the lane. Dad was out with Granddad fixing fences, and he must have spotted me. The grasses were tall, the birds were singing. I couldn't see where I was going. I had a fistful of buttercups I'd picked, and suddenly Dad appeared out of nowhere, the giant that he is. He scooped me from the wild grasses and into his arms. I can still hear him say, 'Where do you think you're going, little girl?'"

She glanced at him through her long lashes, wholesomely honest. "About that time the cows spotted me, too, and Dad held me up so I could pet them. We were surrounded by cattle crowding to get closer. Their tongues kept licking me alongside my head and my outstretched fingers. They ate my buttercups and nibbled on my shoelaces. I laughed and laughed."

Easy to imagine, too.

"That was the happiest I'd ever been so far in my life, cradled in my dad's arms and surrounded by God's creatures with the summer breeze on my face." She shrugged self-consciously as if she'd revealed too much. "It's still my favorite way to spend a day. Out in the fields riding Aggie at Dad's side. If that makes me unlovable, then I don't know what to say."

"Not unlovable. Amazing." Glistening snow melted in her hair like a tiara, and he reached out to briefly touch that snow and her hair. She sure didn't look real, but she was, and so was this moment. A pivotal one he had to get right. "Not every man is man enough to appreciate an incredible woman such as you."

"You can turn on the charm in any circumstance, can't you?"

"It's a gift." She could tease, he could tease. "What's the real reason you danced with me?"

"It's silly."

"If it is, I won't tell anyone."

That earned him a hint of a smile. "Like I said, pity."

"Are you sure you want to fib to an officer of the law?"

"It's not a fib. I do feel sorry for you." Trouble began to twinkle in her eyes. He had a feeling Autumn Granger was a truckload of trouble when she wanted to be—trouble of the best kind. "I wanted to know what it would be like to be in your arms. To be held by you."

Wow. Not the answer he expected, but one that put joy into his very breath. "And? Did you come to a verdict?"

"It was all right." A smile teased at her mouth.

"Just all right? Because it was pretty nice for me."

"Fine. For me, too." She admitted the truth as if reluctantly, but the defenses were creeping all the way down to reveal the real Autumn Granger. The vulnerability behind the tough and breezy cowgirl who carried a .45 and knew how to use it maybe better than he. She lassoed his heart like the country girl she was, a hold that he knew by instinct and faith nothing was going to break.

He cupped the side of her face with one hand. She didn't move away from his touch. His pulse skidded nervously. Would she let him kiss her? He inched closer and she didn't pull away.

A rapid knock shattered the moment. Autumn jumped. He rocked back guiltily into the leather seat as she rubbed her sleeve on the foggy window. A big man glowered in at them from the other side of the door. The smear on the glass might have made it seem ominous, because when the window lowered Frank Granger was grinning ear to ear. "What are you two up to in there?"

"We're talking, Dad. Really." She gave a little huff. "I'm setting the new sheriff straight on a few things, so do you mind?"

"Didn't mean to interrupt. Just wanted to make sure you weren't having truck trouble. Ford, we're driving cattle to the Kents' place tomorrow. We could use extra cowhands if you and that brother of yours would like to ride with us."

"Dad, I'm sure Ford has better things—"

"I'll be there." As if he was going to miss the opportunity. He had a love of Western lore, but Autumn was the reason he said it. She was the reason Frank had offered.

"Great." Frank backed away. "I'll see you at home, little girl."

Ford knew exactly why all the guys in this town, including Denny Jones, had felt inadequate. Not just any man could stand comparison to Frank Granger or understand Autumn's feelings for her father. They were best friends, he saw that now. A lifetime of affection that might intimidate other men, but it inspired him. He felt the same way about his dad. There was nothing more important than family. Nothing greater than love.

"Oh, no." Autumn peered out the window. "Martha Wisener is coming. Out of my truck right now or we'll never hear the end of it."

"Good idea. I'd better go see if my brother has messed up my radio stations." He opened the door and hopped to the ground. Snow went up past his ankles.

"Wait. I didn't get to hear about your long, sad string of rejections."

"There's always tomorrow." He couldn't wait as he closed the door. A whole new life was opening before him, and he felt Heaven shining as he watched Autumn drive away.

Chapter Twelve

The house was quiet with everyone gone. Autumn plunked the truck keys on the shelf by the back door, hung up her coat and stepped out of her high heels. Boy, she was glad she didn't have to wear those every day. She grabbed them by the straps and padded through the empty kitchen. A glow from the living room distracted her. She stuck her head around the corner.

Her dad was sitting there all by himself. The TV was off. Only one lamp was on. He stared at the closed window blind as if he didn't see anything at all. He'd changed out of his tux and looked more like a working rancher in a gray T-shirt and Levis. Something wasn't right. Frank Granger was not a quiet man or a contemplative one.

"Dad? Are you all right?" She padded across the plush carpet. The long hem of her dress shivered around her ankles. She grew more concerned

when he startled just a bit, as if he'd been truly
lost in thought. It had been a big day. Things were
going to be different with Justin married. He and
Rori had built a house on the nearby quarter section of land. Her big brother wouldn't be pounding through the house on a daily basis, stealing
her cookies or taking charge of the remote when
she was watching TV. Was Dad feeling the same
way?

"Just thinking is all." He seemed tired, as if
watching his son marry and the last string of nights
on cattle watch had taken their toll. Keeping a
round-the-clock vigil on the livestock wasn't easy
on the hired staff or on him. "Got a moment?"

"Are you going to bring up the new sheriff?"
She hadn't been born yesterday. She knew how
her father's mind worked.

"We don't have to if you don't want to. Come
sit with me."

As if she could turn down an invitation like that.
She charged across the room and plopped onto the
sturdy coffee table. The new jigsaw puzzle Cheyenne had picked out for the family to do was still
in its box. She nudged it aside. "Are you missing
Justin already?"

"Nope. Glad he's on a flight to Los Angeles.
He works hard and he deserves this trip."

"That's not what I meant, Dad."

"My oldest son just married the best gal for

him." He tried again. Maybe he didn't realize he was dodging the truth. "I couldn't be happier for him. The first of my kids to get married. It's a proud day."

"It's pretty lonely, though. At least until I came home." She phrased it more like a question, knowing full well her tough and rugged father would never admit to a simple human weakness.

"I'm just not used to this house being quiet." He leaned forward, grabbed the puzzle box and wrestled the top off it. "It's something I'd best adapt to."

"What do you mean? I'm here."

"For how much longer?" He flashed his smile at her as he tossed the lid aside and gave the box a shuffle. "With the way the new sheriff's falling for you, you'll be engaged by Christmas."

"Ha! Fat chance." She slipped to her knees and began stacking up the cattlemen's and ranching magazines. "I'm not going anywhere. Besides, Cheyenne will be back to stay when she graduates in the spring. You know Nate wants her to join his practice. Addison has one more year and she'll be home, too."

"That will all be fine." That wasn't what was bothering him, but he could hardly tell her that.

He dropped to his knees on the carpet and plopped the puzzle box between them. A few pieces flew up and tumbled onto the big coffee table. Only then did he notice the scene Cheyenne had picked out: a family on horseback bringing in a fresh-cut Christmas tree on a sled. The snowy hills and forests and the bold blue sky could have been part of their land. It could have been a picture of his family any given year. He could almost hear the children's chatter and occasional punctuations of laughter in the cold crisp air.

He cleared his throat. "Are you going to help me?"

"Sure." She punched the remote and the TV came to life. The news station out of Jackson came on, but Autumn was already checking the on-screen guide. A few pixels winked and blinked as she chose one of their family favorites. *It's a Wonderful Life* came on in mid-movie. Jimmy Stewart started singing under a moon. Frank picked through the two thousand cardboard tabs looking for border pieces.

"Mrs. Gunderson left food in the fridge." Autumn hopped to her feet. "I'll pop something in the oven. Be right back."

"Maybe it's a good time to clean off the satellite." Several more blips were flashing on the screen. Snow was accumulating on the dish. A quick fix. He wanted to finish watching the movie. It would give him something to do until it was his turn to pull guard duty at the line shack tonight. If those rustlers came back, he would be ready for them. He yanked on his boots, zipped himself into his parka and grabbed the broom from the closet.

Snow peppered him as he circled around the house. The fresh air, crisp evening and wide-open feel of his land were comforts that never failed. It wasn't often loneliness troubled him. A man had to be comfortable in his skin to live smack dab in the middle of five hundred thousand acres. It wasn't the fact of his kids growing up and leaving that troubled him.

Cady Winslow was. Sandi and Arlene had both been sending out plenty of signals, but not her. He hiked onto the front porch, put his boot on the top rail and hefted himself up. A few swipes of the broom had snow sliding off the dish. That ought to do it. Now, without interference, he could watch Jimmy Stewart come to appreciate his life.

With the fire crackling in the fireplace and the TV droning in the background, Cady felt cozy and snug as she ladled chicken noodle soup into a bowl. What a pleasant day it had been. She'd stayed as long as she could after the wedding, cleaning up in the kitchen with the Ladies Aid, but she'd come home to emptiness. Maybe she would think about getting a pet. A cat would be nice to purr and curl up beside her on the couch. Or maybe a dog to bark and run at her heels.

For now, she was lonely as she padded in her pink slippers to the living room. The rest of her meal was spread out on the coffee table and she added the soup bowl to it. She sat on the floor and bowed her head. She'd barely finished the blessing when the phone rang.

Great. Someone calling! Her left knee creaked as she got up, circled around the couch and snared the cordless. The familiar number on the screen put a spring in her step. "Adam."

"Hey. I'm in need of a wise woman's sage advice, so I thought I would call."

"I know that tone. What's going on with the girls?" She folded herself on the floor and grabbed a half of her toasted cheese sandwich.

"I can't understand, or at least that's what Jenny tells me." She could picture him shaking his head, perplexed. "What do you know about little girls' fashion?"

"Not too much, but I'm sure I can wing it. What's the big problem?" She took a bite of her sandwich while it was still hot.

"Jenny wants a miniskirt for Christmas, and when I told her she was not putting it on her Christmas list, the end of the world ensued." Adam chuckled self-deprecatingly. "I was informed I know nothing. I stood my ground, but I'm out of my depth. I need help."

"Jenny is way too young for a miniskirt. In fact, I think I am, too."

"It's good to have confirmation. But now I have another problem."

"How did I know?" She put down her sandwich and took a sip of soy milk.

"She wants clothes for Christmas. Fashionable clothes. Things I'm told I don't understand." Adam blew out a sigh. "It's true. My idea of fashion is remembering to put on a tie in the morning. Whether or not it matches my shirt is immaterial."

"Then it's a good thing you know me. I'm a fantastic shopper."

"You're a lifesaver."

"I'm a woman who knows how to use a credit card." She knew that would make him laugh. After finding out beyond all doubt that Frank was never going to look at her differently, she could use one, too. "You could e-mail me her list and I can take a look at it."

"I have a better idea." Adam hesitated. "I don't want to impose, but how would you feel if I invited the three of us over for Christmas? I know you're out there all alone, and the girls miss you. You could help me with shopping then."

"I would love it, but what will your parents say?"

"They won't mind too much. The girls and I

can fly down and visit them on the way home. As long as you are good with it?"

"Good? I'm great. You can see the inn and my little cottage. Oh, and my horse. Little Julianna will love that." This was exciting. She had a fondness for her youngest godchild, who was just ten years old and had a love of creatures great and small.

"It will be good for my girls, too. I appreciate this, Cady."

"Then we have plans to make, my friend."

After making plans to make plans, she hung up, finished her soup and sandwich and got back to work on her jigsaw puzzle. The brief call had been a pleasant interruption, but the house was quiet again. On her TV screen, Jimmy Stewart was saved by an angel. The fire in the hearth crackled and she tried to pretend she wasn't lonely.

This was her life. It was always going to be this way.

Why couldn't she forget the wonder of dancing in Ford's arms even a day later? Autumn tried to focus as she grabbed the pink halter from the hooks in the tackroom. The sensation of security he'd given her had remained at the back of her mind. The smoky timbre of his voice had trailed her through a dreamless night of sleep.

Worse, the peace she'd experienced when she'd

laid her cheek on his chest did not fade. Memories distracted her through her midnight watch when the line shack was cold and silent. She'd nearly let the fire go out. If the rustlers had returned with a dozen helicopters she would have been in serious danger, too lost in a daydream to hear them.

No man had ever affected her like this. He'd been the topic of conversation before Sunday school started. Both Merritt and Caroline had called wanting an update on what they saw as a budding romance. A romance? That thought tortured her.

I'm not falling for him, she told herself. She could be stubborn when she wanted to be. She was tough. She could keep tight control of her feelings. End of story. Letting the man any closer was the quickest way to spell doom.

"You're lost in the clouds today, aren't ya?" A voice startled her, coming as if out of nowhere.

"Scotty." She whirled around, realizing she was halfway across the barn without being aware of taking a single step. Her head was in the clouds, and she needed it with her.

"Suppose you're just tired," Scotty said kindly. A wool cap hid most of his salt-and-pepper hair, and the parka he wore emphasized his barrel appearance. "I could take your shift tonight. Give you a night off."

"We're a hand short with Justin gone." She

didn't mind the late night or hours spent on the job. What she minded was her lack of discipline. When she put her mind to something, she was used to it staying there. *So* not a good sign that she was glancing toward the lane. Ford wouldn't be coming for a while, and yet she was already watching for him.

Sad, pathetic, sappy, she told herself as Scotty went back to saddling horses and she padded down the aisle. The stalls were mostly empty since many of horses were out in their paddocks enjoying the sunshine and snow. A few lingered indoors and nickered as she walked by, hoping for a treat or a pat. Hard not to give in and dole out a sweet.

"Hi, Wildflower." She greeted Cheyenne's favorite mare with a nose pat and a molasses treat, which she pulled out of her pocket. "Were you hoping I was coming to exercise you?"

The mare nickered and tossed her head. She was a sweet mare, used to a lot of attention. Her six-month-old baby pranced up to the gate. Snowflake was already a beauty like her mama with her white and gold pinto markings, snowy mane and big melted-chocolate eyes. The filly stuck her little mouth through the bars and sniffed the interesting bright pink thing. Curious, she dug in her teeth and pulled.

"That's right. It's a calf halter." The back of her neck tingled and she turned around. Ford. How had he gotten here? She hadn't heard him drive in. She forgot to breathe as he strode toward her in silhouette with the sunlight behind him. He could have strolled out of her most secret of dreams.

She could not start hoping he was the one. That any man wouldn't try to change her, could love who she really was. She had to be sensible, dig in her feet and refuse to let hope take wing.

Fine, she was hoping. Just a tiny bit. With every step he took, hope flourished undeniably.

"We couldn't help showing up early," he explained, Stetson shading his face. Could a man be any more masculine without breaking the laws of physics? He knuckled back his brim like a hero of old. "Shay's helping the guy saddle the horses. He's more excited than I am. A real cattle drive."

"It's only a few miles, and we do it all the time."

"Sure, moving herds from winter to summer pastures. This is a big ranch. How do you keep track of your animals?" He joined her in front of Wildflower's stall.

"We spend a lot of time in the saddle. We keep our fences good and except for the occasional mountain lion, we don't have much trouble." Except for the attempted rustling. To her surprise, Wildflower laid her chin in Ford's hands.

"How are you doing, girl?" Gentle, he moved

in. The mare closed her eyes as he caressed the lean lines of her cheek and jaw. Total trust. The man had a way with animals. She could admit it. The hard part was that she admired it, admired him.

"What a pretty girl you are," he mumbled before picking up their conversation. The warmth remained in his words. "I came early because I wanted to see you."

Why did that make the hopes within her take root? *Don't start wishing.* Wishing led to all kinds of disappointments. She fisted her hands, firmed her spine and forced one foot off the ground in an attempt to step away from him. "Why?"

"It doesn't make sense to me, but I missed you." He gave the horse a final pat of attention.

"You saw me yesterday."

"I have a theory if you're interested." Solemn and steadfast, he towered over her.

"I'm not interested in any of your theories, Sherman. You're in my barn, so I'm putting you to work."

"I'm good with that." He didn't seem troubled by the prospect and trailed her down the way.

"We'll see how you do. This is a test. I'm taking Arlene Miller up on her suggestion." She stopped to unlatch a gate to a center pen. The Kents' sick yearlings were looking better. "Hey, there. It's time to go home."

The heifer unfolded her legs, splayed them on the clean straw and struggled to her feet.

"Good job. I brought you a treat." She dug a molasses chunk out of her pocket. It disappeared in an instant. While the animal chewed happily, she slid the soft nylon collar over the heifer's nose and behind her ears. The cow shook her head, ready to bolt, but Autumn spoke in a low and comforting voice. "Hear that? Your ride is here. You get to go home in a truck. Doesn't that sound like fun?"

The calf shook her head, not at all sure about the halter or riding in a truck.

"She doesn't look impressed." He hiked into the pen. Straw crunched beneath his hiking boots. The scent of warm cow and sweet alfalfa was a pleasant combination. Autumn clipped in the lead and handed it to him. He took the nylon rope in surprise. "You don't want me to take her."

"She's only a few hundred pounds. Or can't you handle her?"

"Sure I can." Testing him, was she? Well, he was up to it. He didn't balk at a challenge. As he heard men's voices and the rumble of a two-ton engine echoing through the barn, he didn't need to ask where to take the calf. The animal latched on to the hem of his coat and dug in firm teeth. He had flashbacks to his first day in town and the cattle attacking his Jeep and waving his clothes in the breeze. "Is this a pet or a range animal?"

"You'll have to live dangerously and find out." She walked away, shaking her head at him.

The rustle of her jeans, the clip of her boots and the way her ponytail bounced with her gait filled his senses until he could drown. She had captured him utterly, a storybook beauty in a brown coat and worn jeans who had walked right off the pages and into his life.

Here it goes, Lord. He put it in prayer. *Help me to walk this path You've presented to me as if I'd never been hurt. I have to do this with my whole heart. I don't want to mess up my one chance with her.*

He gave the lead a tug. "Come on, little one. Your ride is waiting for you."

The animal took one look at him, saw that Autumn was gone and dug her hooves into the straw and refused to move. The heifer wasn't so little now. Impossible to strong-arm her down the aisle. Good thing he'd followed Autumn's advice and found time to make a stop at the feed store.

"How about one of these?" He unzipped his pocket, pulled out a treat and held it in front of the calf's nose. When the animal launched forward to snare it, he lured the creature straight down the aisle.

"Ford!" Frank called out. "Glad to see you're

getting the hang of things. We'll turn you into a cowboy yet. Lead her right up the ramp."

"So you're the new sheriff." A gray-haired, lean man tipped his Stetson. "Good to meet you, son."

"You must be Mr. Kent." He landed in the bed of the truck and let the heifer have the treat. He knelt to unbuckle the harness and through the truck's rail slats, he caught sight of Autumn trotting alongside a second yearling.

"What a good boy," she praised as they bounded up the ramp together and she closed the tailgate.

Autumn. She made him see the future. Weekend afternoons spent just like this surrounded by family and neighbors, horses and cows. Love so strong it ached. It was time to put down more roots here. Buy his own horse. Start dating Miss Autumn Granger on a steady basis.

"Not bad, Ford." She climbed over the tailgate. In a split second he was at her side, hand at her elbow, helping her. She didn't need it, but that didn't stop him.

"I try." He hopped down after her.

"I don't suppose you know how to herd cattle."

"I've read about it."

"Sure. I knew that." She led the way into the barn where horses waited in a line, saddled and bridled. "You already know Lightning, so I had

Scotty saddle him for you. Lightning is a trained working horse. He knows what to do. Give him his head. He'll take you through the paces."

"Sounds as if Lightning doesn't need me in the saddle."

"He doesn't, but since Dad invited you I suppose we have to put you somewhere." Not even close to the truth, but she wasn't about to let Ford in on the secret. What nearly happened yesterday in the truck roared back to her full-force. She couldn't forget him leaning closer, intent on kissing her.

"Let me get that for you." Ford reached for Bella's reins and untied them from the iron wall hoop.

Why was she noticing the plane of his chest? The crook between his shoulder and his neck? Because she couldn't forget the pure respite of being in his arms. She tried to escape and bumped into Bella's shoulder. The mare nickered gently, and Ford inched closer. Panic flickered through her in sharp, tiny lashes. She was blocked in. He reached over her to settle the reins into place and wrap the ends around the saddle horn.

She loved that he knew about riding. She liked that he had no problems helping with the cows. She admired the deep blue glint in his gaze as it settled on her. He traced the contours of her face as if he were memorizing them, as if he thought a tomboy like her could be beautiful. He brushed his knuckles against her cheek with tenderness.

"I'm a little sweet on you, Autumn." He leaned in, kissing close. "It's only fair to warn you."

Yes, she was trapped. An answering tenderness uplifted her. He made her care. He'd gotten past her defenses.

"Let's saddle up!" Dad's command echoed through the barn. "Let's get these cattle moving."

The perfect excuse to slip away from Ford, but this time the distance made no difference. She wasn't aware of Dad and Shay mounting up, or Mr. Kent and his son on horseback heading down to take point at the end of the driveway. Every iota of her attention remained focused on the brawny dark-haired cowboy settling onto the horse beside her. Back straight, posture perfect, relaxed as any lifetime horseman would be. He tipped his Stetson to her and rode away like the man of her prayers.

Hold on to your heart, Autumn. She gathered Bella's reins and wheeled her around in the breeze-way. What had happened to the defenses she had built up over the years? They were gone, and she was wide open and vulnerable. There was no barrier between her deepest feelings and the man who rode ahead of her into the promising December sunshine.

She couldn't fall for him. She had to be strong no matter what.

Chapter Thirteen

Ford reined the quarter horse down the driveway. He felt like a hero in a McMurtry novel seeing the cows milling around, smelling the scent of fresh-turned earth beneath their hooves and listening to the ringing moos.

"You and Autumn will take the tail." Frank charged up to him on the back of a powerful dark bay gelding. "You can handle that, Sheriff?"

"I'd sure like to try."

"Any problems, you have your cell phone on you?" Frank wheeled his horse around without touching the reins. "Use it. Autumn, we're under way. Hurry up, girl."

"I'm coming." She trotted down the driveway. The sunlight tumbled over the golden red highlights in her hair and the delicate angle of her jaw.

Looking at her made him fill up with every kind

of emotion. Joy, a sense of belonging and the hope of what was to come wrapped around him. If only his grandfather could see him now. He would have adored Autumn. He would have approved Ford's choice. Beyond all question he knew his parents would cherish her.

"I can't believe you started without me, Dad!" She rode toward him, posting easily in rhythm to Bella's quick trot.

"I can't believe you were dawdling with the new sheriff in the barn," Frank called over his shoulder as he cantered away. "Don't think I didn't see you."

Autumn blushing was a sight to behold. Her jaw dropped in shock, her rosebud mouth made a cute little *O*. Pink as a posy.

He supposed he should take Frank's comment as a sign of approval. That was a good feeling. Nice to know the father and best friend approved.

Autumn was right. Lightning seemed to know exactly what to do. Head up, ears swiveling and nose sharp, the gelding cut to the right lane of the driveway when he caught up with the herd. The large congregation of cattle moved like a black flowing bovine river down the road.

A plump, silver-haired woman came out on the back porch to watch the procession go by. She wore a checked, ruffled apron and a look of interest. He knew just how she felt. This was a Western show come to life. No film could ever capture the larger-than-life feeling of being in the saddle with the wind and sun and the majestic landscape surrounding you. The rock of the horse's gait, the faint creak of the leather saddle and the impact of hundreds of hooves hitting the earth. The living, breathing power of the animals as they pushed and shoved and lowed. He felt smaller than he ever had before, but not insignificant. He was part of something bigger and better. Something good.

He stood in his stirrups searching through the herd. Up ahead he caught sight of his brother. Shay rode toward the front. Hard to see more than his hat and coat in the fray, but he guessed little brother was grinning ear to ear. A dream come true for both of them.

They'd reached the end of the driveway, and the herd swung left to spread out over the paved road. He didn't even bother to comment that they were a hazard to traffic. He kept a sharp eye out for vehicles, but not one came by as they strolled along. Far up ahead the Kents' two-ton truck led the way, with what looked like Kent's granddaughter holding up a bucket of grain in the back of the bed.

"Where do you think you're going?" Autumn charged by him, moving as one with Bella. A half-dozen cows peeled off from the herd, galloping with surprising speed across the front lawn. Ford watched as the stunning woman and her golden mare raced after them, swept around the far side and cut off their escape. The cattle had nowhere to run but back to the herd.

Breathless, he watched her settle her cap on her head as if it was no big deal, all in a day's work. For him, it had been something to see. New respect for her filled him. Hard not to fall deeper in love with her.

"What are you looking at?" She cast him a doubtful grimace, acting as if her defenses were up, but he knew better. She couldn't hide much from him. Not anymore. She guided her horse nearer to him. "Bella does most of the work."

"I wasn't looking at Bella."

"You should be paying attention to the cattle, not me."

"They seem fairly contained." He gestured ahead to the quick-paced mass of cattle eager to follow a grain bucket home. "Especially since both sides of the road are fenced."

"You never know when they might stampede."

"Now you're teasing me."

"Someone has to keep you humble." Humor was about the best defense she could muster at the time. A cow in the back of the herd mooed and shoved the steer in front of her harder.

"What do you mean? I'm a humble guy."

"Oh, sure you are." She rolled her eyes, doing her best to keep every single feeling in check. "You never swagger with overconfidence."

"Hey, I don't swagger."

"Fine, but you *are* overconfident."

"Everyone has at least one flaw." He rocked easily with the horse's gait and looked so fine in the saddle that she wished she could force her gaze away.

"You know exactly how good-looking you are."

"Really? Glad you noticed," he quipped. "I must be making progress. Persistence does pay off."

She clamped her jaw shut before she could say one word to encourage him. *Don't laugh. Don't fall for him. You are just something new to him. A change of pace.* Her fingers curled around her reins until she was sure if she peeled off her mittens her knuckles would be white.

"So, have dinner with me on Friday night." Out of the corner of her eye she could see the devastating flash of his grin. Her defenses wobbled like a tin roof overloaded with snow. She had a fondness for cowboys.

"Friday night is the church bazaar at the firehouse." Thank heavens she had a reasonable excuse.

"How about Saturday night?"

She took it as a sign when the impatient heifer

shied away from the back of the herd and took off at a run, maybe hoping to find a shortcut to the grain. She escaped down the Greens' driveway and Lightning took off, determined to bring in that cow with Ford on his back. Ford seemed to love it, judging by his cowboy's hoot of glee.

Once the cattle were safely behind their newly repaired fences on the Kents' land, the four of them—Autumn and Dad, Ford and Shay—rode back home together. She wished she could say it hadn't been a fun ride, but she would be lying. She swept the last of the pooled water off the concrete toward the drain. Ford had walked the last horse back to his stall; Dad and Shay had retreated to the house to catch the national rodeo finals on TV. The rest of the hired hands were on patrol. A load of towels swished in the washer, and she washed her hands in the sink, glad the horses were cared for.

"I'm getting partial to Lightning." Ford strolled into sight, faintly dusted with alfalfa bits. He appeared taller, if that was possible, and larger in her view. More substantial. He stopped to pet the cow sticking her nose over the top of her gate. "How much does a horse like that cost?"

"Lightning has an awesome pedigree and a competition rating, so probably more than you make in a year." She stopped to rub Buttercup's poll. Too bad it brought her up close and personal with Ford. She felt the rasp of her coat sleeve against his. She breathed in his fresh wintry scent, hints of alfalfa and molasses from the grain.

"Ouch. I could dig into my savings or set up a payment plan."

She knew him well enough to recognize the spark of humor crinkling in the corners of his eyes. "We can always use another hand. You could work it off mucking out stalls."

"I've got experience. Granddad put me to work in the horse barns when I stayed with him. Said it was to build character."

"Sure. As if you shoveled out the barns all day every day." Buttercup's tongue wrapped around her arm as a show of affection. In answer, Autumn ran her fingers down the long plane of the heifer's nose in a light sweep. Buttercup sighed and closed her eyes. Her tongue lolled. She pulled away from Ford's touch and burrowed her long face into Autumn's stomach.

"Aw, I love you, too, Buttercup." She wrapped her arms around the bovine's neck and snuggled her. Love came in all forms. See how full her life was? She had close friends, superglue bonds with her family and enough horses and cows to heap her affections on so that she had no room for anything more. No room whatsoever.

"You doubt my integrity." Ford didn't seem

offended. No, he seemed interested. Maybe he just thought he was interested in her. Maybe she was a challenge to him, and maybe once he'd captured her affections, he would let her down.

He might not be Denny Jones, but Ford had the gift of coming on strong, too.

"It's not your integrity I doubt." She unwrapped her arms from the cow and gave her a treat from her pocket. "You cleaned a few stalls for your grandfather now and then—"

"Wrong." His tone was as light as his step as he hurried to keep up with her. "I had the morning shift at the barns every morning every summer. No excuses, no vacations and no tardiness. I had a pitchfork in hand by 4:30 a.m. and I worked hard until nearly ten. I didn't get paid a dime for it. Grandpop said the reward I got was worth far more than money."

She hiked through the open doors into the waning sunshine. Clouds were rolling in, and that's what she had to do. Summon any obstacle to obscure her growing admiration for the man.

"I tend to agree with him, although I couldn't see it at the time." He kept at her side, his long-legged stride easily adjusting to keep up with her shorter, faster one. "I worked because he asked me to. And because I did a good job, he taught me the finer points of horsemanship. Those lessons have served me well every day of my life since."

"You tell a good tale, Sherman. I grant you that." She climbed up the stair step of bales, ducked her head to keep from bumping on the rafters and pulled on her work gloves.

"It's not a tale, pretty lady." He walked with her the length of the stack to the edge of the top bales. Without her having to ask, he climbed down onto the landing of hay stacked below. He caught the first bale she threw him without so much as a wince. "What I learned from my grandfather helped me to excel at every job I've ever tried my hand at."

"You don't have to convince me of anything." She bent her knees and hefted a second bale by the wire ties. "I'm not the town council. You're not accountable to me."

"I want you to know the man I am." He caught the bale and stacked it in the waiting pickup beside the first. "I hope you are starting to get a clue."

"Maybe you're simply showing me what you want me to see." Heaven knew she'd fallen for that before. She scooped up another bale and tossed it. "There's a whole lot I don't know about you."

"Let's fix that." He stacked the bales neat and tight, just the way they should be.

Fine, maybe his story was true. But that didn't mean she had to be foolish. Her defenses might be down, but she had her heart to protect.

"Ask me anything and I'll tell you the truth." He

caught another bale and stacked it, fast and efficient. He was ready when she tossed him another one. "Any question."

"I get the burnout factor. That's why you left your last job." She was getting warm, so she unzipped her jacket and got back to work. "Why did you take a position with our town?"

"The pay was right, I liked the idea of a slow-paced, forty-hour-a-week job, which I'm still holding out hope for. And when I drove here I saw more horses grazing along the way than at the other two towns I interviewed with." He didn't break a sweat as he kept stacking. "I didn't come here to escape burnout as much as I came to find dreams I'd lost along the way. Maybe discover new ones."

She felt the brush of his gaze to her cheek and she flushed. "Really, do you think I'm going to fall for your cheesy lines?"

"Worth a try."

She could fall for his grin, too. If there was one man on the planet who could make her want to risk trusting again, it would be Ford Sherman with his strapping good looks, work ethic and catching smile. She was accumulating quite a list of his features she adored. Didn't that spell doom?

"Guess I need to try harder," he quipped, standing on the tailgate to stack the last row of bales. "Quick, I need to think of some cheesier lines."

"Yes, that is *so* going to work." *Don't laugh at him*. It would only encourage him.

"I'm not as suave as you think." He slid the last bale into place and hopped to the ground. "I have to work really hard to come up with those lines."

"Pathetic." She accepted his hand to help her down. Not that she needed it, but she didn't want to be rude and refuse him. If a warm ribbon of respect curled through her at the contact, then she could ignore that right along with everything else she was feeling. "At least I'm starting to understand the long string of rejections your brother mentioned."

"We're not back to that again, are we? Quick, let's change the subject." He whisked open the truck door for her.

"Not a chance. You know all about my heartbreak. Now it's your turn." She lifted her chin in a challenge. "It's only fair."

"Life isn't fair."

"No, but I had hoped you were tougher than that." She leaned against the truck. "How about just one rejection?"

"You're enjoying this. I can tell by your sparkling eyes." He planted his hand on the truck beside her. She wasn't ready for him to move in, but he wanted to. "Those big hazel eyes make a man want to fall and keep falling."

"I thought you were done with the cheesy lines."

"It's a habit at this point. I don't know if I should apologize or keep going. Maybe one of them will eventually work on you." He hid behind humor so she wouldn't guess how badly he wanted her to trust him. "I'm not going to give up."

"I'm thinking of hobbling you and leaving you in one of the calf pens," she joked.

Did she feel this, too? A terror that ripped through with the speed and power of a tornado? She'd been hurt. Was that the only reason she was fighting him so hard?

"Do you think this is easy for me?" His gloved fingertips brushed the side of her cheek.

"You look as if everything is easy for you." She didn't move away from his touch. "You urban dudes have more ego than I've seen in ten country boys combined."

"Is that right?" Funny that she thought so. "It's not ego. Just fascination with you."

"Fascination. That's exactly what I'm afraid of." She probably thought she'd hidden the flash of pain in her eyes, but she didn't. "Everything is new here. You've said how much you love all things Western. How much of what you feel is the thrill of seeing ranch life firsthand instead of in a book? How much of your enthusiasm toward me is a part of that?"

"So, that's what you think." It was clear now. "You think I'm carried away and confusing that with feelings for you."

"Relationships and me don't mix. They don't last." The sunlight chose that moment to fade into the grayness of a storm. Tiny flecks of snow danced through the sky to alight on her hat, her hair, her shoulders.

Why didn't she know how amazing she was? Couldn't she see herself as he did every time he looked at her? He knew how tempting it was to hide behind what had happened in the past because of fear. But the only thing that did was limit the future and steal the wholeness of the present moment. He'd learned that the hard way. He had his share of regrets like anyone else.

He wanted no more lost chances. He took a deep breath and gathered his courage. He let down his walls. He laid down his defenses. Pure vulnerability was hard, but he could do it.

"My last girlfriend dumped me right after I proposed to her." He spoke past the pain that haunted him years later. "I made mistakes, I grant you that. I worked too many hours. My job wasn't nine to five, five days a week. I can be stubborn, and I could have listened better. I know that now. But I did the best I could in the relationship at the time."

"What happened?"

"Jemma left me for a lawyer, pawned the ring and I never saw her again." He winced. Muscles in his jaw tensed. "She was a gorgeous woman, almost as stunning as you."

"Are you ever going to stop with the charm?" She arched one eyebrow, skeptical.

"I'm telling the truth as I see it. She was too gorgeous for me. My buddies on the force kept trying to tell me I was dating out of my league and I wouldn't be able to keep her, and they were right. I was devastated and I felt like a chump because I didn't see it coming. It hurt enough that I stopped dating. Stopped believing there was good in a woman. I never want to get hurt like that again."

"I'm sorry." She meant it. She knew how deep hurt could go.

"But I'm doing it all over again, or don't you see?" Snow sifted between them as airy as grace, making him appear blessed. Adamant. Righteous. "Except this time I've fallen faster and harder and further than I thought I could go. I'm in love—"

"Love?" That word made her panic. She wasn't ready for love. Like, yes. Definite, serious like, yes. But love? That was a dangerous word. When a woman believed in love, she was setting herself up for disappointment. That's the way romance had turned out for her every time.

"Yes, in love," he emphasized and cupped her face with both hands. "How about we do a little experiment to find out?"

"Like a questionnaire?"

"Like a kiss."

"You've got to be joking." She would not allow him to get any closer to her. So, why wasn't she moving away? Not a yard, not a step, not even an inch. She wasn't breaking his hold on her. She wasn't pushing his hands away from her face. Her pulse skipped three beats. "No kisses. I'm not ready for that."

"It's for purely practical purposes." His eyes darkened with unmistakable kindness. He angled close and his nose bumped hers. "If one of us doesn't like it, then we can file this in the fool-hardy category."

"It will be foolhardy either way." She curled her hands around his wrists and held on when she should be stepping away.

His lips settled on hers in the sweetest kiss she had ever known. It was a perfect movie kiss, the kind where stars would blink to life and birds burst into song. His kiss made hope dawn within her and joy brush her soul. That one moment in time was flawless, but it could not last forever. He lifted his lips from hers and his mouth curved into a tender grin.

"Definitely foolhardy." His thumb caressed her cheek. "But I have my answer. How about you?"

"I'll get back to you on that." She could gaze into his eyes forever. There she saw his honest feelings. No man had ever looked at her as if she were his princess.

She was smart enough to know he was caught up in the moment. She had to hold on tight to her heart. She had been caught up in the moment, too, but it had been a mistake. That kiss should never have happened.

Her phone rang, a cheerful electronic jingle. She reached into her pocket, cleared her throat and tried to sound normal. "Hi, Dad. What's up?"

"Tucker's going to be on in a few minutes. Get the lead out and come watch him compete. He just might win this."

"We'll be right there." She pocketed the phone and closed the truck door. "Looks like hauling hay will have to wait."

"I'm good with that," he quipped. "I'm in no hurry to unload that truck. I forgot how heavy hay bales are."

"Then you're in luck. Your job is done for the day." She launched away from the truck, taking the lane in a fast walk. She tossed over her shoulder, "Are you coming? Keep up, cowboy. *If you can.*"

"I'm right with you." His gait didn't falter as he caught up and matched her stride. He would follow her anywhere.

Chapter Fourteen

Mrs. Gunderson met them at the back door with steaming cups of hot chocolate topped with melting marshmallows. "He's almost on. Oh, this is so exciting."

The kitchen smelled like gingerbread cookies. Autumn felt Ford's hand settle on her shoulder comfortably, as if he thought she was his girlfriend. He'd already used the *L* word. What was next? Fear lashed through her as she woodenly accepted one of the housekeeper's ceramic mugs.

It was just a kiss. That was all. No need to panic.

"He's up!" Dad's call echoed through the house. "That's my boy."

"Last year Tucker washed out before the finals." She managed to keep her hand still enough so the cocoa didn't slosh over the brim. Now if only

Ford would remove his hand from her shoulder she would be good. She padded into the living room. "He's had a good run this season."

"I had a chance to meet him at the reception," Ford explained to his brother, who slouched in a recliner with his eyes glued to the widescreen. "He's a good guy."

"Sit down, you two." Dad scooted over on the sectional. "He's in the gate."

She edged her mug onto the coffee table. Mrs. Gunderson slipped a plate of oven-warm cookies nearby, grabbed the hem of her apron as if with nerves and slipped behind Shay's recliner to watch.

Sure enough, there was her brother on TV, knees up and hunkered down on a bareback bronc. The grandstands flashed across the screen in full Technicolor. The commentators remarked in surround sound on Tucker Granger's skills. In the chute, he gave his belt a hike, tightened his grip and raised his fist.

Autumn's heart stopped, as it did every time. *Keep him safe, Lord. If he falls, help him to land softly.* The gate opened and the bronco charged out into the arena head down, rear hooves kicking at the sky.

"He's doing it!" Dad steepled his hands as if he'd finished a prayer or was in the middle of one. "Look at that horse go. Tucker's almost there. Three more seconds. Two—"

Off Tucker flew, tumbling into the dust and into the way of the horse. Still in a bucking frenzy, the animal trampled him. Autumn covered her eyes. Ford's hand landed on her shoulder, offering her comfort she so wanted to take. If only she could block out the gasps of horror from a stadium full of spectators or the words of a commentator. "He's down. He's hurt. This is a terrible turn of events for Tucker Granger. The paramedics are starting to work on him. What do you think, Bill?"

"Oh, God." Dad's choked words were the beginning of an otherwise silent prayer.

She could not look. She kept her eyes covered, wishing the drone of the commentators would stop. She heard the distinctive tap of cell-phone buttons. Ford left the room. The rumble of his voice drifted in from the kitchen.

How was Tucker? She peeked through her fingers. On the screen, an EMT crouched over her brother's body giving chest compressions. She squeezed her eyes shut. Beside her Dad was muttering the Twenty-third Psalm.

Lord, don't let this be real. This can't be happening to Tucker. He'd just been here, full of laughter and life, her little brother. The bane of her existence growing up. He'd pulled pigtails, stolen schoolbooks and stood up for her when she'd needed it. *Help him, please.*

"You can look now, girl." Dad sounded shaky. Every bit of color had drained from his face. "He's going to be okay. We gotta believe that. He left me an emergency number somewhere."

Autumn slid her hands away. On the TV an ambulance flashed away, and the focus returned to the commentators, whose words never reached her. Another horse was in the chute, and the rodeo continued. All she could hear was the rushing in her ears. She was on her feet without realizing it. The world had turned fuzzy and surreal, as if she were walking through a dense fog.

"I've got the only available seat on a plane leaving in sixty-eight minutes." Ford pocketed his phone on the way to the back door. "We can make it if we hurry."

Dad grabbed a small duffel bag Mrs. Gunderson must have packed. "The airport is an hour away."

"That's why they gave me the flashing lights."

"Then let's hit the road." Her father made a bee-line to the back door and flung it open. "Autumn, are you gonna be all right here?"

Her father's gaze searched hers, so full of hurt and fear and worry for Tucker that she didn't dare add to it.

"Fine." She prayed she sounded convincing. Frank nodded once before turning away. The nanosecond he was out of her sight, tears flooded her vision. She wished the hand that curled around the back of her neck wasn't Ford's. She wished it wasn't his strength she leaned on for one brief moment, but it was. She didn't want to need him as his lips brushed the crown of her head, and then he was gone, too.

Snow had been falling hard for over an hour as Ford made his way down Mustang Lane. The country road was one long, untouched sheet of white as he navigated around a lazy corner and slowed to a crawl. He searched through the dark for the small reflector on the Grangers' mailbox pole. When he spotted it, tension rolled off him. Almost there. Almost to Autumn.

Halfway to the airport, Frank had been able to talk to the hospital about his son. He'd been taken to emergency surgery, and whatever the doctor had told Frank had made him heavy with grief. Ford hadn't prayed so hard in a long time, since Granddad's final illness. He didn't need to stop and ponder that. The Grangers already felt like family.

The ranch house's main floor glowed lemony in the dark. He parked by the garage, zipped himself into his parka and hiked up the garden path. Hard to believe there was strife at all anywhere in the world with the snow tapping down peacefully in every direction like nature's symphony. A porch light led the way to the back door, which swung open before he could knock.

"Bro." Shay's face was red from the cold. "We just finished up feeding. It was like being in an old Western. Except for the bales instead of haystacks. Oh, and the truck instead of a wagon."

"Being with Autumn is like having the Old West come to life." But that wasn't why he loved her. He crowded into the mud room to shake off the snow and searched for her with a need he couldn't explain.

Autumn. The instant his eyes found her standing at the fireplace, relief hammered through him. She appeared smaller than the invincible cowgirl he was used to. She didn't turn toward him. She faced the hearth, holding out her hands to the crackling warmth. Her straight shoulders slumped, as if it took all of her considerable strength to hold herself together. His feet carried him to her.

"We just got a call from one of Tucker's rodeo friends." Mrs. Gunderson set a pan of Swedish meatballs on the table. "He's going to stay at the hospital until Frank can get there. It's still touch and go, the poor boy. Autumn, honey, supper's ready."

His hand settled on her shoulder. "You need to eat something."

"I know." She set her chin, apparently determined not to need him, because she spun out of his touch. It did not stop his devotion to her. She took a shaky breath, as if fighting hard to keep it together. "Thanks for driving Dad and for finding him a flight."

"I wish I could have found one for you."

"No, someone has to stay here. Scotty can run things, but we're stretched too thin on patrols as it is." She padded around him, seeming so distant. "I don't want to put him in that position if the rustlers come back. I can always hop a flight if Dad really needs me."

"You can trust me to help out here." He followed her to the table, but his brother and Mrs. Gunderson had already vanished into the living room. He caught sight of TV trays and heard the murmur of the rodeo. They were probably watching in case the commentators announced any updates of Tucker's condition. "I can fill in on the patrols. Shay and I can help with the ranch work."

"I can't ask you to do that." She shook her head so hard, her ponytail whipped back and forth. "You've done too much for this family already."

"Do you think I mind?" His hand curled around her elbow, holding on when she wanted him to let go. Every fiber of her being screamed at her to put a safe distance between them, but she didn't move. Her feet refused to cooperate.

"I'm glad to be here. I plan on always being here." He moved closer and made the rest of the room shrink.

"That's what men always say." She'd learned this the hard way. "I haven't had so much as a wink of interest from anyone in so long, you have to understand why I don't believe you." *Or need you. Or want to rely on you with everything inside of me.* She curled her hand around the back of her chair, needing to hang on to something because it could not be him. "I'm sure you mean it, Ford, but in time you will feel differently."

"Just goes to show you don't know everything." Winter thunder booming through clouds couldn't sound nearly as sure as the man. "I've been alone a long time, too. I've been lonely, and I had lost hope. Then I saw you ride in like a Western heroine and I thought, *She's out of your league, Sherman.* But did that stop me?"

"You should quit your job and write novels." She grasped at humor, the only weapon she had left. She could not be drawn in by the intimate vulnerability in his endlessly blue eyes. She had to stay resolute. "You can sure make up whoppers."

"I know what you're up to, beautiful." He cradled her face in his hand, his touch so tender he had to be part dream. "You know I'm an honest man. You know I've fallen so hard for you, I'm never going to find solid ground again."

"I'm afraid that's what you think. For now. You mean it, for now." But it couldn't possibly be true, she could not give in. "You don't know what the future will hold."

"No, but I have an intrepid heart. I don't scare easily. I don't quit often. When I see something true and good, I want to hold on to it. On to her."

How did she keep her common sense now? She wanted to believe. She really did. She wanted to pull him close instead of push him away. She wanted to be uplifted by hopes and dreams. Maybe that's why she let his lips brush hers in the sweetest kiss. His kiss was better than any wish, it felt like a promise kept. As if any happiness were possible.

When he lifted his lips from hers, he did not move away. "How about you?"

Good question. She was not strong enough. Too much could go wrong, and it was too much to lose. She was better off standing on solid ground, believing true love could not happen to her, than disappointed a second time. That's what men did. They disappointed you. And you were left to pick up the pieces and pretend you weren't as crushed as you really were.

She hiked up her chin, tossed him a breezy look and did her best to act unaffected. "I can be fearless, but I'm never foolhardy. I'm not sure which category you fall into."

"That's fair enough." He brushed a curl from her face. "Let's get some food and you can tell me what you need Shay and me to do around here."

"I like a man who knows who's boss." She didn't step away, but kept her hand fisted in his shirt, holding on.

"I don't have problems taking orders from a lady." Dangerous dimples dug deep. "You'll know why when you meet my mom."

"And exactly why would I be doing that?" She arched one brow defiantly.

"Because my folks are coming out this weekend. Dad wants to see my new digs, and Mom wants all of us together for Christmas." He tucked the wayward curl behind her ear. "My family is like yours, or haven't you noticed?"

"You don't strike me as a family man."

"Then you haven't seen me." He ignored the flash of disappointment as it sliced through him. What he couldn't ignore was the way she became distant without moving a muscle.

"I'm afraid I see you all too clearly." She walked out of his arms and away from his embrace, unaware of how much pain she caused him.

"No, Addy, I don't think you should leave school." Autumn did her best to focus on the phone conversation as she rode her workhorse along the perimeter of the pitch-black field. Holding her cell with one hand and a high-powered flashlight with the other, she signaled Aggie to stop, stood in her stirrups and eased the flashlight beam along the section of fencing. Intact and no sign of tracks anywhere. "Dad promised me he would call Cheyenne with any news, and she will call you."

"Why am I always the last in line?"

"Because God saved the best for last, baby sister." She relaxed into her saddle and pressed her heels gently to Aggie's sides. The horse plodded forward, head up and alert as if she were looking for trouble in the dark, too.

"I feel as if I should *do* something. I want to help." Easy to imagine Addy in her dorm room in her fuzzy flannel pj's, with a book on her lap. "I'm going crazy with nothing to do."

"What about prayer?" Autumn shone the beam along the next length of fencing. It was good. Instead of returning her attention to the conversation with her sister, her brain looped straight back to her conversation with Ford before dinner.

Then you haven't seen me, he'd said in a tone that sounded sadder every time she remembered it.

"Autumn?" A faraway voice penetrated her thoughts. "Yoo-hoo. Earth to Autumn."

Addison! She shook her head, wondering where

her common sense had run off to. "I'm sorry. Would you say that again?"

"Not until you tell me how things are going with Ford. Pretty well, considering you've hardly heard anything I've said. You're totally into him, aren't you? You're falling for him."

"I do not fall." That's why she was good at her work. She knew how to keep her saddle, but if she was thrown, she knew how to tuck and roll. A girl always had to be prepared. And in the case of Ford Sherman, caution was the better part of valor.

A beep in her ear startled her. Another call. Panic licked through her. "Addy, I have to go."

"If it's Dad, you call me. You tell me what he says!"

She clicked off and the incoming call rang. "Dad?"

"No, it's just me." Cheyenne. "Have you heard anything?"

"Not since Dad called after he landed." Aggie turned toward the line shack, taking the last section of fence slow because of the shadows. The horse understood the work better than Autumn did sometimes. She flashed her light, and the beam illuminated perfect barbed wire strung up without a break.

"I'm worried sick. There's a flight leaving in the morning. I could be in Nevada by noon. Maybe there's something I can do." Worry made her words thin and wobbly, but there was exhaustion, too. Cheyenne put in long, hard days. Any long break from her schooling could put her back.

"Do what Dad says and stay in school. We'll pray there isn't a single reason why you need to miss your classes." Pray. It was about all she'd been doing this evening aside from poring through her Bible. Those familiar and treasured words had calmed her as the night progressed and there had been no reassuring call from Dad. As much as she wanted to be with him, she was glad she was here to run the ranch. At least that was one thing her father wouldn't have to worry about.

"Tucker is still in surgery. It can't be good. There was internal bleeding, and all I can think—"

"Don't think. Just pray." Aggie nickered to get her attention. The horse seemed to be staring intently at something up ahead in the dark. Autumn swung her flashlight across the sleeping herd of cattle to the inky shadows on the other side of the open-air shelter. Nothing. She flicked off the beam and let her eyes adjust to the night. "I've got to go, Cheyenne. Do yourself a favor and get some sleep. Dad will call when Tucker's out of surgery safe and sound. You'll see."

"Positive thinking. Gotcha." Cheyenne clicked off, leaving Autumn alone again.

Normally she might unsnap her saddle holster

and draw out the Winchester, just in case. This time it was a hazard of another kind approaching. She turned Aggie toward the trail. Flurries brushed against her cheeks and eyelashes as she gazed through the night. Far down below shone the faint glow of the porch light. A man's silhouette crossed in front of it.

"Ford, you're early for your shift." Her words echoed in the silence. All of nature was asleep. "It's only about midnight."

"I know we agreed on two o'clock, but I wanted to see you." He rode into sight as if part of the shadows, powerful even in the dark. He'd willingly given up a good night of sleep in a warm house to watch over her cattle. It wasn't because he was the sheriff, because Dad had asked him to help or because he thought there would be something to gain.

No, Ford was simply being honest, which he'd been all along. He'd meant those things he'd said to her. He did have an intrepid heart. He didn't let a little thing like below-freezing temperatures or his own comfort stop him from showing how much he cared for her.

"Have you heard from Frank?" He reined Lightning to a stop outside the small cabin and swung down.

"Not yet." She dismounted, too. "Starting to really worry."

"It will be okay. Have faith. Hebrews 11:1." He patted Lightning's side affectionately. "It's one of my favorites."

"Now faith is the substance of things hoped for, the evidence of things not seen," she quoted. "Mine, too."

The few feet separating them felt like a mile. Part of her wanted nothing more than to lay her cheek against his chest. To listen to the reliable thump of his heartbeat, close her eyes against his granite strength and simply be. To lay down her loneliness, the independence she used like a shield to protect herself and accept his love.

But she could not. "I appreciate that you're here. You could be sound asleep, snug and warm right now."

"Instead of freezing my fingers off. Let's get the horses sheltered." He took Lightning's bridle bits. "Around back?"

Her phone rang again. She tugged it from her pocket. A gasp escaped her when she saw her dad's number.

"I'll take care of Aggie." Ford snared the reins from her and disappeared into the darkness, leading both horses with him.

Her hand shook so badly she couldn't hit the right button. After the second try, the call connected. "Dad?"

"Tucker made it through surgery. He's in

recovery now." Dad blew out a pent-up breath. "I got to see him for two seconds. He's unconscious and pinned and stitched up, but he's alive. They plan to move him to ICU in a bit."

Thank you, Lord. Gratitude filled her until her eyes smarted. "Have you told the others?"

"I'll get to it now. Just wanted you to know first. Did Ford make it there tonight?"

"We're up at the southeast line shack." Tucker was okay. That's what mattered. The shock and tension gone, suddenly she was too cold. She shivered. Her teeth chattered. Overwhelmed, she blinked hard until her eyes were dry.

"...he's a good man," her dad was saying. "I feel better that you're not alone."

"Don't you start matchmaking," she warned him. "Me and Ford are not meant to be." She held out her free hand to the wonderful heat. It began to chase away the chills and the numbness. "He's not the one for me. He never will be. Got it? Nothing is ever going to change my mind."

The door creaked, the only sign she wasn't alone. She glanced over her shoulder just in time to see a shadow disappear into the dark. She could feel the sting of his hurt in the icy air. Ford had overheard words not meant for him.

"I gotta go, Dad. Call Cheyenne and then get some sleep."

"Will do."

The call disconnected, the fire popped and snapped greedily and she didn't know what to do. Did she go after him? Did she apologize or try to explain? She grabbed the doorknob, unaware she'd crossed the small one-room cabin until the cold air chased away the fire's heat from the front of her clothes.

Maybe this was for the best. Ford would finally stop trying to ask her out on a date. He would stop torturing her with those impossibly dreamy kisses. He would give up on her, just the way he would do eventually anyway when his interest faded or when he realized she would always want to work alongside her dad and brother, that she always was going to train horses and raise cattle and she wasn't going to give up what she loved just to be loved.

Not even for a great man like Ford.

Boots crunched in the snow outside, startling her. Wasn't she alone? She expected to hear the steeled strike of horse hooves as he rode Lightning down the hill. But Ford towered in front of her, a great hulking bear in his parka and winter gear. She stumbled aside, not believing her eyes.

"I made a promise to help, and I'm keeping it." He brushed by her as cold as the night. He set a packed saddlebag on the wooden chair by the fire. "You may as well get on home. Consider yourself officially relieved for the night."

"But I—" Apology tangled in her words.

"It doesn't matter." He cut her off and held his hands out to the fire. "It's not like you tried telling me. It's okay, Autumn."

"I just feel so—"

"Don't." That would only make it worse. He kept his back to her so she couldn't see the truth. "I'm a big boy. I can handle rejection. You've had a rough day, so go get some rest."

Silence settled in between them as she hesitated, probably debating whether to argue or to leave. The shuffle of her boots on the floorboards marked her decision.

"Thanks for staying, Ford."

"Sure. No problem." His heart was breaking, but he was just fine otherwise. He listened to her boots striking the floor and the squeak of the door as she closed it behind her. He waited a few breaths before following her.

She'd disappeared from sight but not from his affections. Those remained, cracked and bruised. Since he was alone he hung his head and fought the pain he wanted no one to see.

Chapter Fifteen

❧

"Good afternoon," sang the cheerful hospital volunteer as she sailed through the open door to the private room.

Frank looked up from his book, amused at the way his son managed to show enough signs of life to toss a smile to the young lady. Three days in intensive care and now one day out and the boy was able to turn on the charm. That had to be a good sign if there ever was one. Frank was grateful for it after sitting through sleepless nights at his side, praying for his beautiful little son.

"Hi, Tucker, you have even more flowers today." She carried in two bouquets. "You must be well liked."

"They're pity flowers, mostly. Folks feel sorry for me, likely as not." As weak as he was, Tucker managed to get one dimple to show.

Frank shook his head, set down his book and

got off his duff to help the poor girl. He sure hoped she wasn't buying it, but she turned rosy and giggled. He took a look at the arrangements on the cart in the hall, spotted his son's name on a couple of cards and grabbed them. Balloons bumped and floated behind him as he hauled it all into the room.

"And there's one for you, too, Mr. Granger." The girl sailed away from Tucker's bedside. "Did you see it?"

"Can't think of anyone who'd send me anything." The words were out before he realized that wasn't true. Sandi and Arlene came to mind. Dread filled him as he plopped Tucker's arrangements on the windowsill. Available space on the remaining surfaces was going fast.

"See? It's for you." The cheerful gal thrust a vase at him and swept away. "See you later, Tucker. You feel better."

"I'll do my best, Brittany." Tucker managed to get both dimples working in fine order.

That boy. Frank settled the collection of white and yellow rosebuds on the edge of the sill and plucked the card from the plastic holder. The TV blared to life, buttons clicked as Tucker worked the remote, and Frank squinted at the writing on the note because he refused to admit he needed glasses.

Frank, I'm sending prayers for your beautiful

boy. May God watch over you both. And it was signed simply, *Cady*.

The starch went out of his knees. Air whooshed out of him until he couldn't remember how to breathe. He blinked. How about that. He would never have guessed in a million years a big city girl like Cady Winslow could understand. She'd spent her life building an impressive legal career, according to what he'd overheard, and she had never married or had children of her own. Yet she knew what his son was to him, a precious child he loved so fiercely and truly he could still see the little boy in the grown man. That he would have rather been on the floor of the arena in his son's place.

Maybe Cady wasn't as different from him as he'd figured. She might not be as disinterested as he thought. A lick of joy blew through him.

"What you do have there, Frank?" He hadn't heard the crisp tap, tap of heels on the tile behind him, but he heard it now as his sister-in-law barreled into the room.

"Nothing I mean to share." He pocketed the card.

"Dad got flowers from a lady, and I bet I know who." Tucker might look as pale as could be and bruised and battered, but his heart was still beating. "I think he deserves his privacy, don't you, Aunt Carol?"

"I most certainly do not. Who would send Frank flowers? Ooh, that's going to torture me, but I'll get to the truth of it, just you wait and see." She cast a merry smile as she plunked a cup of steaming tea on Tucker's bedside table. "There. Anything else I can do for you?"

Frank's cell rang, so he grabbed it. Looked like Addison calling in to report on how her last final exam went. That meant she was ready to leave for the airport and fly home. Home. Gratitude filled him. They would be together—the whole family—for Christmas. He felt optimistic as he hit the button and greeted his littlest daughter. Yep, life was mighty good. He had God to thank for that.

"Now it's starting to feel Christmassy!" Addison announced as they drove into town. Dark had fallen and the main street sparkled with silver stars, golden ornament balls and striped candy canes hanging from the streetlight poles. Garlands adorned shop windows and wreaths hung on doors closed for the night. "I love this time of year. Everything is so festive."

"You're in a particularly good mood." Autumn slowed to the required twenty-five miles an hour at the library and crept past the church. She doubted Ford was out with his radar, but no way did she want to get pulled over. He'd been avoiding her ever since he'd accepted the truth, but having to face him up close was one humiliation she wanted to avoid.

She steeled her emotions, gripped the steering wheel more tightly and kept a sharp eye on the road.

"I'm just glad my finals are over and I aced them. Yes!" Addy punched the air with one first. "I'm free to do whatever I want. And don't say it. I know you want to put me to work in the barns, and that's okay. But remember I've had a really tough time with all my studying, homework, papers and tests. I deserve a few days off. Do you think Mrs. Gunderson knows how to make fudge?"

"If she doesn't, I'm sure she can find a recipe and wing it." This end of town was as quiet as could be, but up ahead lights flashed and blinked and a long line of parked cars hugged the curb.

"Ooh, what's up at the fire hall?" Addy strained against her seat belt to get a better look. "It's not the church bazaar, is it?"

"Probably," she said vaguely. Was that Ford's Jeep? She peered over her steering wheel, realizing it was.

Ford. A terrible tangle of emotions clutched her and refused to let go. She wasn't in love with him, so why was she feeling horrible because she'd hurt him and terribly empty because she missed him?

"Stop! Please? I want to get a bag of candy from

Santa." Addy pointed to a parking space along the sidewalk. "It will only take a minute."

"You're too old for Santa."

"But I'm not too old for candy." Addy used her Bambi-eyed look.

Impossible to say no. Autumn found herself steering to the curb and cozying into a parking spot right behind the sheriff's rig. Of course. Pain slammed into her, and she did her best to ignore it, just as she'd been doing for days. She shut off the engine and pocketed the keys, staring at the string of Christmas lights twinkling over the open bays of the station. Ford would be inside. How was she going to handle it?

Like she'd been doing the last handful of nights. Keep her distance. She'd pretended she hadn't seen him riding the fence line in the dark, waiting as long as it took for her to abandon her post at the line shack, saddle up and ride Aggie home. Distance was the key to keeping the pain away. She could survive this as long as she kept the length of the room between them.

Any help You want to give, I would appreciate, Lord. She grabbed her purse and hopped onto the sidewalk. Christmas music met her ears and the low roar of conversations led the way into the brightly lit fire hall. Since the town had yet to raise money for a second truck, there was an empty bay, and it was filled with tables and tables of homemade items, all to raise money for the church's giving tree.

Doris spotted them first amid the throng and waved both hands as if she were trying to scare off a herd of elk. "Girls! I'm so glad you could make it. I feared the worst when I didn't see hide nor hair of you. How's Tucker doing today?"

"Fine, considering." Autumn noticed how her sister gave Doris a hug and kept on going straight to the tables full of pretty homemade things to buy. "Dad called a while ago. Sounded as if Tucker is already back to his normal self. Half the nursing staff is in love with him."

"What are you girls going to do about Christmas?" It was Martha's turn to amble up.

"Tucker is supposed to be released in a few days. Dad and Aunt Carol are driving him home." She couldn't wait to see for herself that her brother would be fine. She couldn't wait for Dad to get back. She missed his steady, easygoing company. "I'd better go keep an eye on Addy. Look, she's already getting into trouble."

"Autumn, do you have any money?" Addison held up a quilted book cover. "I love this. I have to get it, and I'm broke."

"You know what Dad says. If you can't afford it, then you don't need it." She didn't want Addy to think she was a pushover.

"But I need it. I really do. Okay, that's not true. I need two."

"Here's twenty." She pulled two tens out of her purse. "That's all you're getting."

"Thanks, Autumn. You wouldn't happen to have another ten?"

Fine, so she was a pushover. She handed over a third bill, left Addy happily shopping and did a fast scan of the area. She saw a crowd of women debating over items on the tables and a queue where Arlene Miller was taking money, but no sign of Ford. That was a major relief. He was probably in the back room giving out candy along with the mayor, who dressed up as Santa every year. Good. That meant it shouldn't be hard to avoid any run-ins with the sheriff. She would stay out here and he could stay in there. She could continue denying the truth.

"Autumn?" A satin-smooth alto startled her from her thoughts. Cady wove her way through the crowd and into sight. "I'm so glad you came. I've missed you."

"I've missed you, too." And it was true. She let Cady slip an arm around her in a quick friendly hug. She'd had to cancel their riding lesson last week. Funny how accustomed she'd gotten to seeing Cady so often. "How is the new designer working out?"

"Better than I could have expected, especially

since she has to drive out from Jackson every morning." Cady lit up. She clearly loved her work with the inn. Her gentle green eyes glittered like emeralds, and her delicate features softened in the most luminous way. She swept a lock of brown hair behind her ear. "We're actually ahead of schedule. The rooms are taking shape. It's starting to look homey."

"And thoroughly classy, I'm sure." Knowing Cady's understated elegance, her inn would be a breathtaking place of comfort and beauty. "I can't wait to see it."

"I'm taking up the suggestion of having an open house. You and your family are on the guest list." Cady grew serious. "How is Tucker?"

"The doctors say he'll fully recover to return to rodeo riding and be trampled by a horse again," she quipped. "Well, they didn't say that exactly. It was—"

"—your dad," Cady finished, growing faintly pink. "It sounds like him."

"Yep, that's my dad, the comedian." She missed him. And if there was another man whose presence she was missing, she did not have to think about it. Where had Addy gone? She couldn't spot her sister anywhere.

"I'll keep my prayers coming," Cady promised. "If there's anything you need, or if you need to talk, call me. Got it?"

"Thanks. That means a lot." She squeezed Cady's hand and she felt instantly as if the shadows inside her were not as bleak. It had been a long time since she had longed for her mother or anyone in that role she could look up to. It felt good to know Cady's friendship was there. "I'll see you at the Christmas Eve service?"

"I wouldn't miss it." The older woman tilted her head, as if listening. "Oh, Martha is calling me. I'm supposed to be helping Arlene. Take care."

"You, too." Alone again in the crowd, Autumn headed for the door. Knowing Ford was in the next room made little stabs of regret lodge in her midsection. She wished she could take back what she'd said, but she couldn't. And it wasn't even true, she realized. Her emotions were tangled up so thoroughly it was hard to tell exactly what she felt. Just because she wasn't ready to leap without looking didn't mean she hadn't come to care about Ford.

Even if she didn't want to care about him.

She waved goodbye when Doris called out to her and stepped onto the shadowed sidewalk. It felt colder here alone, and she wrapped her arms around her middle, holding her parka closed. Her breath rose in great clouds, and she tried to block out the realization she'd come to.

She wished she could get a do-over for that one moment in time. She would go back and erase those words that had hurt Ford. She didn't want to let another man disappoint her and try to change her. So why did she want to fix things with him? Why weren't her feelings listening to her head?

She plucked her key ring from her pocket and sorted through it for the truck key. A movement across the street caught her attention—a familiar Jeep. Ford's rig had moved and was now angled in front of an old Ford Falcon, elderly Mrs. Tipple's car. The Falcon's hood was up. It looked like she had engine problems, the poor lady.

Quick, get in the truck. Get off the street. But her feet weren't obeying. She stood rooted to the sidewalk as Ford strode into sight. Her brain cells screeched to a halt. Her nerve cells lost their ability to fire. Her entire attention was riveted to him as he lowered the Falcon's hood.

"There you go, Mrs. Tipple. I've got you running again." Had he always seemed that strong and sounded as kind? "You drive straight home, and if you have to stop, don't turn off your engine. I'll give your son a call and let him know to get that battery changed."

"I don't know how to thank you." Frail Mrs. Tipple leaned out of her rolled-down window. Her silver curls framed her adorably wreathed face. Even at Autumn's distance it was plain to see her gratitude. "You're a good man, Sheriff Sherman."

"It's my pleasure to help, ma'am." Ford tipped his hat like a cowboy of old.

Her heart tumbled and fell helplessly. Ford had accused her of not seeing the man he was. He'd been right. Why could she see him clearly now? She tried to shuffle her feet forward, but her neurons continued to misfire. *You know what the problem is, Autumn Granger. You've destroyed any chance with him, and so the fear is gone.*

Fear had clouded her vision. It had kept her from seeing what was right in front of her. Regret wrapped around her like the cold night air. She'd always thought of herself as fearless. In her life she'd chased off cougars hunting Granger cattle, she'd faced armed cattle rustlers and wouldn't hesitate to put herself in danger to protect anyone she loved. But when it came to opening her heart, she'd failed.

The back of her neck prickled. She realized Mrs. Tipple had driven off while she'd been lost in revelation, and Ford had spotted her. He didn't move a muscle. Just towered like he was made of granite, staring but not speaking. The street separating them felt like an impossible rift to cross.

It's too late, a voice in the back of her head told her. She'd taken the safe path and look where it had led her, right back where she started. Alone.

"Autumn?" Addy clattered onto the sidewalk, her purchases and Christmas candy in hand.

"There you are! I scored some great stuff and some candy canes, too. They had a whole lot left over. I got you some."

"Th-thanks." The word came out scratchy and raw. Across the street Ford turned his back, a deliberate act. The temperature suddenly felt colder.

"There's Ford. Hi, Sheriff!" Addy called across the street, perpetual motion and merriment. Across the street Ford lifted a hand in response, but he didn't turn around. The unyielding plane of his back said it all.

The keys slipped from her wooden fingers and crashed to the concrete. She knelt to grab them, hating that it took time away from her escape. She yanked open the door and dropped into her seat. Behind the barriers of the glass and the steering wheel, she felt somewhat shielded.

"So, has he asked you out on a date yet?" Addy yanked her belt and buckled it. "Inquiring minds want to know."

"I haven't said yes." That was the truth. She doubted she would get another chance. She plugged the key into the ignition and the engine roared to life.

"You should go out with him." Addy tore into her sack and plucked out two peppermint hard candies. She handed one over. "He's a lot like

Dad, don't you think? He's got that strong, kind, honorable thing going on."

"He does." It had taken her forever to see it. She checked for traffic before pulling onto the street. Now that she believed him, Ford no longer wanted her.

It took all her willpower not to glance in the rearview mirror for one last sight of him as she drove away.

He'd never known pain as deep as the hit he took every time he saw Autumn. Ford stumbled in the dark of his bedroom, yanked on a thermal shirt and rummaged for his warmest sweatshirt. He did his best to ignore the fact that he'd come close to crossing the street earlier in the evening just to talk to her.

You are a man who doesn't know when to quit, Sherman. He pulled on a second pair of wool socks and padded down the hall. His parents were in the second bedroom, and he didn't want to wake them. They'd flown in today and had loved everything about the area. It felt good to have them here. Mom was already making noises about buying a Christmas tree and hunting down all shopping prospects in the area. He saw a trip to Jackson in his future, which would be fun. Maybe they would take a family ski trip to the resort and make it an event.

"What's up?" A sleepy voice slurred in the dark living room.

"Nothing." Ford sat down to drag on his hiking boots. "Go back to sleep."

"You goin' to the Grangers'?" Shay sat up on the couch, which he'd been relegated to since there wasn't a third bedroom in the house. He rubbed his eyes. "I could come."

"Forget it. I need someone who can stay awake." He grabbed his coat from the small closet by the door. "I didn't know it was physically possible for you to open your eyes this early in the morning."

"What time is it?"

"A little after one." He shrugged into the garment.

"Boy, you must sure like her."

That was putting it mildly. He zipped up and went in search of his hat and gloves. He found them along with his keys. He didn't know if he was stubborn or just plain dumb, but Autumn was shorthanded and he'd sworn to pitch in. His brother emitted a loud, long yawn and dropped back into his pillows. Ford wished he could do the same. He opened the door and stepped into the cruel cold. A few quick steps took him across the porch and onto the walkway. Since he'd given his folks the carport for their rental car, he had ice to scrape off his windshields before he could get on his way.

He hit the remote to unlock the doors, and that's when he noticed the flat tire in the front. Strange. The tires were brand-new, right along with the vehicle. He squinted through the dark at the rear tires, but he already knew what he would find. Slashed, just like before. He thought of the aerial maps he'd been studying on all of Wyoming and the reports of other incidences in three states, all using a helicopter and cattle trucks on section lines. Only big ranches were hit in all cases. The rustlers were methodical, careful in their research and smart in their execution. They didn't have qualms about shooting first. And they were back.

That meant Autumn was out there alone. The only other help she had were the two other ranch hands in the line shacks over a mile away in either direction. They were stretched pretty thin. Fear licked through him, threatening to turn into panic. He fought it and glanced around. The cows in the field drowsed, motionless humps in the darkness. This was the problem with having cattle for neighbors. He glanced in the direction of the garage— the Plums. He turned on his heel and, running all-out, fished out his phone and dialed.

No answer. Autumn's cell went to voice mail. Frustrated, he ground out a message. "Someone cut my tires tonight. Looks like the same kind of knife the rustlers used on your family's rigs. Keep an eye out. They are going to hit tonight."

He shot into the house, fighting a bad feeling in his gut. Was Autumn all right? Did his warning come too late?

Please God, let her just be screening her calls. Please.

"Get up, Shay. Pull on some pants. Quick." He flipped on the kitchen light and punched in the phone number Velma had written down for him. The Plums were good neighbors. He was about to find out exactly how good.

Chapter Sixteen

With no moon to see by and no moon to guide her, the night felt ominous and potent as it did before a powerful storm hit. She'd been unsettled enough so that she'd taken Aggie out on another sweep of the field. Louis in the northeast line shack had called to report the Angus herd was restless. Probably nothing more than a cougar nearby, but he had a bad feeling.

She had one, too. The Herefords had been asleep thirty minutes ago and were now on their feet, milling around. The bull scented the wind, his head up and ears alert.

"Hey, Clancy." She dismounted and held out her gloved hands. The bovine ambled up to her and burrowed his face into her abdomen. He was a gentle giant, a calf she and Dad had bought at auction and raised from a bottle together. She'd tumbled instantly in love with the snuggly little baby with the big doe eyes. She could still hear her father's rumbling laughter as they taught the calf to drink from a bottle. That had taken a few tries because the little guy would butt the bottle with all his might and it would fly out of her hands and land anywhere—in the next pen or in the aisle. It even bonked Dad in the head.

She missed her father. She was used to turning to him for guidance or help. He was a consummate rancher, and she still had much to learn. If he were here, she wouldn't feel quite as alone. The night stretched out endlessly in a pitch-black void, and she didn't know if it was her instincts warning her or her own fears troubling her. No one could read cattle like Frank Granger, but she'd picked up a thing or two from him. It was her turn to be in charge, her responsibility to make the right decisions for the animals who trusted her.

She thumbed her phone from her pocket. Clancy squinted at it curiously as she glanced at the screen. The LCD came to life. Excited by the glowing gadget, his tongue shot out, and he tried to steal it from her.

"Sorry, buddy." She rubbed his cheek, but he stomped his front hoof, perplexed by why she would not share. She gave him a treat from her pocket instead and he chewed happily, jowls working, but his ears remained up and alert.

She frowned at the screen, ignored the new

message icon from Ford and dialed the house. Thick silence had settled across the land. Not one owl hooted. Not one coyote howled in the hills.

"'lo?" Addy answered on the fourth ring. "Autumn?"

"I want you to make some calls for me." She watched as Clancy twisted to face the Kents' property, miles away. "Call in the rest of the hands. They are officially on night shift pronto. Louis, Scotty and I are out here all alone."

"Will do!" Addy slammed down the phone.

"What do you think, Clancy?" She laid her hand on his shoulder. He leaned into her touch, as if needing her comfort. She stared down at the screen and winced. Should she listen to Ford's message? He was canceling out on his shift tonight. Why else would he be calling at one in the morning? Disappointment hit her. She'd pushed him away. She couldn't fault him, but it hurt. Seeing him earlier on the street with his back to her, a cold unbreachable wall, hurt, too.

A feeling deep down urged her to listen to the message, but could she put herself through hearing his voice? Of thinking about what might have been if only she'd had more courage?

One of the cows began to moo, and the others joined in. That was definitely not right. She scrolled through her electronic address book and hit the number for the Kents. No answer. The bad feeling multiplied in her stomach. She went to dial the Parnells when Aggie gave a nervous nicker.

"You hear something, girl?"

The mare stood at alert, too, as if waiting for her to mount up, so she did. Time to check the fences again. As long as they weren't cut, the animals weren't going anywhere. She wheeled Aggie toward the line when Clancy charged in front of her, head down like a rodeo bull on a rampage. The shot rang out before she could react. Clancy kept charging into the dark, Aggie kept cantering and she was still in her saddle, so the bullet had to have missed.

She pulled the Winchester from the saddle holster and hit the safety. Her arm was strangely shaky as she aimed. Adrenaline coursed through her until she didn't feel the biting cold on her face. Time slowed as she looked through the scope trying to trace the line of fire back up the hill. A sniper was up there, and she had to find him before he fired again. Frantic, she searched the inky shadows. Nothing.

A little help, please, Lord. She saw the flash before gunfire rang out. Aggie's rocking gait, the dull heaviness in her arm and the knowledge that she was alone against armed men fell away into nothingness. She sighted, exhaled and squeezed the trigger. The rifle kicked hard against her shoulder.

That she felt. It radiated down her arm, up her neck and through her ribs in one great crash of pain. Funny how firing the rifle had never felt like that before. The Winchester was a big firearm, but it had never felt like a hundred-pound lead weight. Her arm buckled, and the rifle came to a rest across her lap. Something warm and wet was spreading along her shirt. When she looked down there was a dark, coin-shaped stain on her parka.

She'd been shot. Nausea gripped her stomach. Her head went fuzzy and woozy. Tiny tremors rolled through her. Not exactly convenient at the moment, because she could see Clancy disappearing into the darkness. She heard a thud as he ran into something or someone and realized another sound had replaced the cattle's mooing. A helicopter banked, coming in to drive the five hundred head of cattle out of their field.

"Oh, no, you don't!" She dropped Aggie's reins, shifted the rifle to her left shoulder and squinted through the scope.

The beat of the blades grew deafening as the helicopter bellied over her, dipping low to take a position closer to the ground. If she took out the rotor the way Dad had, she could bring them down. The tip of the rifle kept bobbing. Her right hand trembled. She had to keep it steady.

Concentrate. She dug deeper for a reserve

of strength. Gunfire popped, bullets whizzed and chunks of dirt flew. She blocked out her fears, the Winchester steadied and the safety lights near the blades slid into the crosshairs. She squeezed the trigger, and the gun's kick knocked her out of the saddle. She fell. The ground came at her hard. She hit, bleeding again from another bullet, and she couldn't seem to breathe.

Defenseless, she watched the helicopter swing low and close in. The gunman kneeling at the open door took aim. She was exposed, an easy target. A single shot rang out.

Ford. Her thoughts arrowed straight to him. She longed for him so intensely she actually could see him hovering over her, a perfect dream. One last desperate wish. Ford, the one man she needed. Love for him filled her and brimmed over. Too late now to change what had happened between them. Overhead the helicopter sputtered, which was strange since she'd only winged it, and smoke rose against the velvet sky.

The dream in front of her moved and dropped to his knees at her side. "Autumn? Can you hear me?"

Maybe he wasn't a figment of her imagination. He was here. He'd come just like he'd promised. She opened her mouth, but no sound came out. She felt cold and oddly weightless. Air rasped in her throat. She couldn't seem to breathe in it or out. Scary, but his hand curled around hers, holding on tight and giving her strength.

"Hal's going to stay with you." Ford moved out of her field of vision.

No. She didn't want him to go. She needed him. She wouldn't be all right without him. If only she didn't feel as if she were drowning, she might be able to tell him that. Pain slammed into her like a speeding semi. She heard Ford as if from a far distance. "That's it, Hal. Keep pressure on both wounds. No, harder. Don't let up. The county helicopter is minutes away."

"I'll do my best, Sheriff." Hal Plum eased onto the ground, looking in charge. "Don't you worry, missy. I was a medic in World War II. I've got an eye for these things, and I say you're gonna be just fine."

She still couldn't breathe right. She rolled her head to the side. She caught the last glimpse of Ford, gun out, racing through the night. What a big man he was, and not just of stature. Someone was with him, and it took her a second to realize he'd brought his brother to help.

Something nibbled her forehead. She recognized that whiskery velvet muzzle. Aggie lent her support as the helicopter struck ground somewhere close enough and hard enough to rattle the earth. The last thing she heard was Hal saying, "Stay with me, missy," before everything went black.

Chapter Seventeen

Frank had a lot to be thankful for on this Christmas Eve. His son was home safe and sound and currently under Mrs. Gunderson's watchful care. His daughter had been released from the hospital with enough sass and vinegar that she'd insisted on attending the candlelight service. He'd had a nice chat with Ford earlier in the day, and it looked like a few nice changes would be coming her way.

He was proud to sit with all three of his daughters, mighty beautiful little girls in his opinion. His precious son Justin and his Rori had come back from Maui glowing with happiness. The rest of the family—his brother, sister-in-law, nieces and nephews—crowded together on the bench in the next row. Even nephew Pierce was back from a tour in Afghanistan and had brought his lovely wife, Lexie. It was nice to have everyone gathered, a blessing of the best kind.

As the minister ended the last prayer, Frank added one of his own. *Father, thank You for watching over my family. I am truly grateful indeed.* He loved nothing more on this earth than his family. There was never a better time to be thankful for his abundant blessings. Not much was missing in his life. Just one thing.

He did his best to keep from turning around in the pew and searching for Cady. He'd wondered what she was doing for the holiday. If Autumn and Tucker hadn't needed him he would have taken the time to invite her over for the family festivities. Maybe he could find her after the service and make sure she wouldn't be alone. Asking her to Christmas dinner might be a fine way to start off things with her.

The choir began to sing the first strains of "O Holy Night." This truly was a divine night, the night when Christ was born. He put his arm around Autumn, who was looking a little pale. He shouldn't have let her come, but he'd always had a hard time saying no to the gal. He was proud of her. Often, the most important achievements in a person's life were quiet accomplishments of the heart and spirit. He was thankful when the choir silenced and the service came to an end. He'd had about all the emotion a man like him could take.

"Autumn." A woman appeared in the aisle.

Martha had a knack for parting crowds. "I'm so thankful you are safe and sound. What a scare you gave us all."

"I couldn't let Tucker outdo me." Autumn managed a breezy answer, but Frank protected her casted arm from the tussle of the folks in the aisle. "The sheriff is the one who deserves the credit. He brought in the rustlers, not me."

"To hear tell it, you were the one who did all the shooting." Martha marveled at the notion. "I think we have ourselves a humble sheriff. I'm going to have a word with him about that. We want the facts straight for the newspaper. Did you hear the other good news?"

"What might that be?" Carol nosed in. His sister-in-law had abundant curiosity.

"Little Owen Baker is in the hospital, too. Sierra took him there during the dinner rush." Martha, glad to be the center of attention, gave a little wave to Sandi Walters as they squeezed through the vestibule. "He had one of his breathing problems at the diner, and Cady Winslow and her good friend from New York were there having supper. Turns out he's a big fancy cardiologist, and he came over to talk to Sierra. Turns out it might not be his lungs at all. Can you imagine? Just goes to show our Doc Thomas is slipping. He's getting old."

"And you and I aren't?" he teased gently as they squeezed through the vestibule. He would remember to add little Owen to his prayer list tonight. He also hoped he was hiding his reaction to the other bit of news. Cady had a friend? Martha had said "he." A man had come to stay with Cady for the holiday?

Five kinds of disappointment battered him. Of course, a classy lady like her would be spoken for. No wonder she had always been reserved around him. She had an involvement. Those flowers she'd sent, well, he'd been the one to misinterpret the message. He had no one to blame but himself for the defeat sinking him.

"In fact, there he is." Martha charged ahead, waving to get a tall, dark-haired man's attention, but the bustle of folks spread out in the parking lot was noisy, and the man must not have noticed her. He was conversing pretty intently with Cady.

All Frank could see was the woman, happier than he'd ever noticed before. She was, as always, prettier than a picture wrapped up in a tailored wool coat with her full brown hair done in some fancy do. Radiant and amazing. Too bad she was out of his reach.

"Autumn!" Two girls ran up chattering and squealing the way females tend to do. He glanced over long enough to recognize Merritt and Caroline hugging his daughter. His gaze boomeranged back to Cady Winslow. Too bad his wishes did, too.

"Aunt Cady!" A little girl around ten or so bounded up, all sweetness and curls, and clung to Cady's hand.

Aunt Cady. The light went on. Disappointment slid away, leaving one giant hope. These folks were her family, he realized. Now that he could make himself look at the other guy, it was plain to see the man was somewhere in his mid-thirties or so. Far too young to be an adversary for her hand.

Family. How about that? He found himself grinning wide. Looked like he was still in the running for Cady's heart. As for his plans to invite her to the family celebration, there was always next year.

"Are you all right, Dad?" Autumn asked, the note of concern unmistakable.

"I'm fine. Just tired." That was the truth. Between worrying over his kids and his cattle lately, he was tuckered out. "It's been a whirlwind."

"I can't argue with that. On the upside, I think things will be a lot quieter from here on out."

They navigated the icy spots on the sidewalk together and crossed the street. Cheyenne and Addison trailed a few paces behind. Rori and Justin followed. They were Dad's ride back to the house. She could not wait to get home. Christmas was her favorite time of year. Tonight they would warm eggnog and sing a few rounds of Christmas carols at the piano before calling it a night.

"You girls drive safe." Dad opened the truck's back door and helped her hop onto the seat. She was moving easier these days. The bullet wounds to her upper arm and to her lower chest were on the mend. Soon she would be back to her usual self, riding Aggie, caring for the cows and training her horses. For now she was content to relax in the leather seat, wave goodbye to her dad and let Cheyenne take the wheel.

"Now it's feeling like Christmas," Addy said after they were on the road awhile. "I spent all morning decorating the tree—"

"While I was out taking over Autumn's chores," Cheyenne pointed out.

"And then Mrs. Gunderson and I made Christmas cookies." Addy beamed. "I haven't done anything like that since Aunt Opal left us for Arizona. I had so much fun, and Mrs. Gunderson really knows how to bake. She showed me all these hints. That's something a mom would do."

"It sounds nice," Cheyenne agreed. "Mrs. Gunderson fusses over us. I like that."

"I do, too. She's a keeper." Autumn had been on the receiving end of their new housekeeper's fussing. Homemade chicken soup, lots of her favorite food and little pampering touches she hadn't had in her life in a long while. "She is very motherly. It's nice."

They fell silent at the pain they shared at having lost their mom long ago. Their aunt Opal had tried to fill the void for them, but only a mother really could. Not that a twenty-nine-year-old woman actually needed a mom, but the thought of one was incredibly nice. After all, she had caught the respectful longing in her father's eyes as he watched Cady Winslow in the after church crowd.

Lord, I hope my dad and Cady find true love. She sent the prayer heavenward and not because she wanted a mom. Her dad needed someone great to come into his life. He didn't deserve to spend the rest of his time alone.

"It is nice," Cheyenne was saying. "I got a whiff of those homemade rolls she baked for our dinner tomorrow, and I—uh-oh. Lights. Something's wrong up ahead."

"I hope no one is hurt?" Addy worried.

Those weren't just any lights, but red and blue strobes. There was only one lawman on this side of the county.

She wasn't aware of the truck slowing to a stop or of unbuckling her seatbelt or hopping into the snow. She didn't feel the icy air against her face. Her pulse thudded in her ears as she followed the shine of the headlights. The sheriff's Jeep was angled across the road. A tall, broad-shouldered man's form merged with the shadows, and he wasn't alone.

"Having trouble, Sheriff?" she called out above the clomp of a few dozen hooves on pavement.

"These cows wouldn't happen to be yours, would they?" Ford Sherman strode into the beam of headlights, a great, towering, impressive man of honor and might.

"No, sir." She met him in the fall of light and strained to glance at the cow's flanks. "That's the Parnells' brand."

"I saw the family in church tonight. Figure they'll be coming along shortly." He gestured to the small bag of treats he'd spread out on the shoulder of the road. "I guess I should have got a bigger bag. They're almost gone."

"And I don't have any cookies with me." She shoved her good hand into her pocket, shivering. In the quiet moments at the hospital and in the more relaxed ones at home she'd had a lot of time to think about what she wanted to say to him. So why weren't the words coming?

Because she was scared again. Scared he wouldn't want her, he wouldn't forgive her, that she'd missed her chance. When she rehearsed what to say, she'd been confident instead of unsure, steady instead of trembling. The words hadn't tied up on her tongue the way they did now.

"It's good to see you out of the hospital." He looked distant. Not as cold as when he'd turned his back to her on the street, but just as remote. "You probably don't remember what happened after you took that second bullet."

"I remember you." Striding in like her own personal hero. Standing tall and mighty, a stalwart man to the core. The biggest, greatest man she knew. Feelings she didn't want to acknowledge fluttered to life within her. Sweet feelings, tender feelings threatened to tear down her defenses for good. "You saved the day. You saved me. The doctors told me I would have bled out if no one had helped me."

"It was all Hal's doing. He's the hero."

"Not to me." Humble. Why hadn't she seen that about him along with all his other awesome qualities? She was seeing them now. Gravity didn't seem to have a good hold on her as she leaned against the Jeep's fender closer to the man she respected. "What are you doing out here, cowboy?"

"It's a twofold trip." He leaned against the rig next to her. "I came to bring your dad a check. He and I have been in negotiations for Lightning. As of today he's mine."

"Dad sold Lightning? He didn't tell me that."

"I asked him not to. You had enough on your mind just recovering." His voice dipped low, layered with hidden emotions. "You gave me a good scare. The last thing a man wants to see is the woman he loves hurt bad. It gave me some much needed perspective."

"Perspective?" It *was* too late. Devastation crashed through her. Every unspoken hope she had dashed to the ground. He was going to reject her. Losing him once hadn't been bad enough. He had to make it good and final. Make it clear he no longer wanted her. She straightened her spine and gathered her dignity.

"I saw the woman I loved being carried off in the sheriff's chopper, and I didn't know how bad you were hurt. But a hit in the rib cage is never good." He crossed his arms over his chest like a barrier.

"It was a few broken ribs."

"It was worse than that. I can't tell you the torture I went through having to stay behind. I had to deal with the rustlers and wake the mayor for the cell keys and all the while I didn't know how you were. I'll never forget sitting in the waiting room with your dad later that night and praying for good news."

"It turned out all right. Or, it will as soon as I heal." She tilted her head, cuter than any one woman had the right to be. Fragile wisps escaped her braids, framing her silken cheeks. So very vulnerable. "You still care about me?"

"Maybe a bit." He closed the distance between

them by catching her hand. There was nothing like the sense of rightness he felt as her fingers twined between his. "To be completely honest, maybe I care more than a bit."

"I had a perspective change, too." Hard to believe she was opening up to him, but her hand tightened within his, clinging hard enough to make hope beat in his chest.

"What kind of perspective change would that be?" He felt as if he couldn't breathe waiting for her answer.

"That maybe you're not so bad for a city boy."

"Glad you think so." He leaned in a little closer. She might think her affections were sealed up tight, but he could see them. The starlight dusted her with gentle platinum light, exposing the wish on her face. A wish that matched his own. He took a steadying breath because taking the next step wasn't easy even for a man like him. "I wanted to see you tonight."

"You did?"

She really had no idea how deep his affections for her went. Deeper than the infinite black sky. Brighter than all the stars in God's amazing heavens. She was his greatest prayer answered. A rare love for all time. He turned toward her. The munching cows, the fact that her sisters were watching from the truck and the worry that her father would be driving up any instant faded away.

Nothing mattered but this perfect moment. The one that might change his life forever.

"I have something for you." He reached into his pocket and pulled out the small black jeweler's box. "My dad proposed to my mom on Christmas Eve, so I thought I would keep up the tradition."

"You're proposing?"

"Sure." He removed the ring from its nest. An impressive oval diamond glittered in the starlight. "I want you to know that I never gave up. My love for you has never wavered. It has done nothing but strengthen every time I look at you. Every time you look at this ring I want you to know beyond all doubt I will always love you."

"You seem awfully sure that I will say yes." The panic returned in little frightening flutters.

"When I asked your father's permission to marry you, he seemed to think you would accept." He knelt before her, her left hand cradled in his.

She gazed at the man kneeling honestly at her feet, blessed by stardust, his entire soul laid bare. She'd kept waiting for him to disappoint her and he'd never done it. He'd never let her down. He was the man who never would. Even when she'd pushed him away and made it clear he had no hope he'd still been there for her, dependable and true.

Just let the fear go, she told herself. *Believe.*

"Autumn, I already love you more than I thought

it was possible to love." Never had a man been more sincere as he pressed a kiss to her hand. "I can't wait to see how much more I will come to love you as the years go by. Will you be my wife so we can find that out together?"

His proposal touched the fragments and cracks of her heart and made it whole again. She felt Heaven's reassurance whispering in the breeze as absolute joy chased away every ribbon of fear. "Ford Sherman, I would love to be your wife."

"Love?" He questioned that word as cool gold slid onto her finger. He rose to tower over her, blocking out the night sky, filling her entire vision. "How long have you loved me?"

"Maybe from the first moment I spotted you." She laid her hand on his chest, full of ardent devotion. Beneath her palm she felt the reliable beat of his pulse, and a rope lassoed her heart, binding it to his. She knew that as strong as she was, he was stronger. He could be the man she turned to, the man she could depend on, the man who loved her for who she was. She laid down her last defense. "Maybe I loved you before we met. I feel as if I've loved you always."

"Always. I like the sound of that." His smile became a kiss. The gentlest brush of his lips to hers, and her soul responded. Storybook endings could happen to a girl like her. In the sweetness of his kiss, she saw their future. A small-town wedding. Walking down the aisle on her dad's arm. A happy marriage and children to come. Horse rides and cattle drives and family Christmases with the entire Granger clan.

A cow mooed, and she realized they had a problem. Amused, she laid her hand on Ford's shoulder. "Turn around," she urged, doing her best not to laugh.

The cows had eaten all their treats and had turned to gnawing on his four-wheel-drive. One cow tried to pry the leather off the steering wheel. Several were licking the side door hard enough to remove paint. One heifer proudly held up the duct tape she had peeled off the side view mirror.

Their laughter mingled in the night. Star shine made everything flawless and new, a perfect world of possibilities as Ford laid his arm around her shoulder. Justin's truck pulled up with Dad in it and the Parnells right behind them.

"This is the strangest Christmas Eve I've ever had." Ford pulled her into his arms with tender reverence. What a nice place to be.

"Welcome to the Granger ranch." She wrapped her good arm around him and held on tight so bliss wouldn't carry her away like a balloon in the wind. "Maybe you want to come to the house for Christmas. Bring your family, too."

"We'll be there with jingle bells on," he quipped. Her sisters tumbled up to congratulate them. Her dad winked at her with pride in his eyes. The Parnell girls found some candy in their SUV to lead the cattle down the road.

"I guess it's time to go home." Ford opened the Jeep's door.

Home. How good that sounded. Tomorrow there would be roasted turkey with all the trimmings, family fun and more memories waiting to be made. For right now, there was just the two of them beneath a starry sky, alone as the rest of the vehicles drove away. Ford's diamond winked on her left hand, a symbol of his never-ending love.

"We're going to be happy. I promise." His lips found hers.

"We're going to be more than happy," she whispered against his kiss. "We are going to be happily-ever-after."

A sense of rightness lifted her up, and she felt Heaven smile.

* * * * *

Don't miss Jillian Hart's
next Inspirational romance,
HIS COUNTRY GIRL
available from Love Inspired.

Dear Reader,

Welcome back to Wild Horse, Wyoming. I hope you enjoyed getting comfortable and revisiting the Granger Family Ranch. In the snowy beauty of the breathtaking landscape, you can feel the gentle country breeze on your face, hear the cattle calling and find peace. As you know, a few things have changed since Rori and Justin's book, *The Rancher's Promise*. Frank tried to figure out if he had a chance with lovely Cady. Justin and Rori got married, and a sheriff moved to town. Amid all this, Autumn Granger was trying to get her ranch work done. She never fathomed how true love would come in the form of a big-city vice cop.

I wrote this story from my heart and from my experiences of growing up in the country. I've hidden several childhood memories in these pages—small-town weddings, the church's Christmas bazaar and even an affectionate bottle-raised bull. It's why the Grangers' stories feel like home to me. It's my hope you feel the same way. I also hope you liked how Autumn and Ford's journey brought the true love God meant for them.

Wishing you the best of God's blessings this Christmas season,

Jillian Hart

QUESTIONS FOR DISCUSSION

1. What are Autumn's first impressions of the big-city sheriff? What does this say about her character?

2. What is Ford's reaction when he first sees Autumn? What does this tell you about his character? How do you know he is sincere?

3. In the beginning of the story Autumn wrestles with fear. She is afraid to trust in love again. How does she overcome this? Have you ever felt this way? How has it affected you, and how have you handled it?

4. Why doesn't Frank ask Cady out? What is he afraid of? Why is she shy around him? What is she afraid of?

5. What role does the community of the town play in the story? How does it help develop the romance? What Christian values does it show?

6. Why does Autumn agree to dance with Ford at the wedding? What new part of her character does this reveal?

7. What do you think are the central themes in this book? How do they develop? What meanings do you find in them?

8. How does God guide both Autumn and Ford? How is this evident? What do they learn about their faith?

9. Autumn fears that no man will love her just as she is. How is this challenged through the book? What causes her to change?

10. What role do the animals play in the story?

11. Do you perceive Ford differently as the book progresses? What do you see? How do you know he will be happy staying in Wild Horse?

12. What do you like most about Ford and Autumn as a couple? How do you know they are meant for each other?

13. What is the story's predominant imagery? How does it contribute to the meaning of the story? Of the romance?

14. There are many different kinds of love in this

book. What are they? What roles do they play in Autumn and Ford's romance?

15. When does Autumn finally believe true love can happen for her? What does she learn?

LARGER-PRINT BOOKS!

GET 2 FREE
LARGER-PRINT NOVELS
PLUS 2 FREE
MYSTERY GIFTS

Love Inspired

Larger-print novels are now available...

LILP10R

HISTORICAL

INSPIRATIONAL HISTORICAL ROMANCE

Engaging stories of romance,
adventure and faith,
these novels are set in
various historical periods
from biblical times
to World War II.

NOW AVAILABLE!

Steeple
Hill®

For exciting stories that reflect traditional values,
visit:
www.SteepleHill.com